AFTERSHOCK

RACHEL HATCH BOOK SEVEN

L.T. RYAN

with

BRIAN SHEA

LIQUID MIND MEDIA

THE RACHEL HATCH SERIES

Join the LT Ryan reader family & receive a free copy of the Rachel Hatch story, Fractured. Click the link below to get started:

https://ltryan.com/rachel-hatch-newsletter-signup-1

Love Hatch? Noble? Maddie? Cassie? Get your very own Jack Noble merchandise today! Click the link below to find coffee mugs, t-shirts, and even signed copies of your favorite L.T. Ryan thrillers! https://ltryan.ink/EvG_

ONE

"GET A LOOK AT THAT VEHICLE." CLYDE HICKS WIPED A FILM OF FLAT Pepsi off his upper lip. "Meth heads, am I right?"

Darren Lawson followed the gaze of his partner. The vehicle was three cars ahead of Hicks's gray Ford Taurus. Persistent rain pelted the windshield. Nothing new. Lawson wondered why he'd traded the warmth of Austin, Texas, for frigid Anchorage, Alaska.

"Why not turn the wiper on?" his partner Darren Lawson asked.

"Let the rain camouflage our position. It'll be easy enough to spot our target. Harder for them to spot us." Hicks was full of useful tidbits and in the few months since Lawson had been attached to the Fugitive Task Force, Hicks had done well to teach him all the tricks of the trade.

Even if that meant sitting in the pouring rain with the car off.

"You mind if I kick the heat on for a quick minute?" Lawson asked.

"This guy is gonna pop smoke and disappear if he walks out of that bar and sees a car idling."

Pop smoke.

Hicks always used terms from his military service. Lawson had never served and occasionally had to sneak a Google search on his phone to figure out the meaning.

"I'll be fast," Lawson replied.

"Not worried about him running as much as I am about him fighting. He's got a body on him. At least one that we know of. Court dismissal or not, make no mistake, we're hunting a murderer. And to me there is no greater threat. Guys like him aren't going to go easy. They would rather shoot their way out and die in a blaze of glory than see themselves behind bars again."

"Aren't we too close?" Using the side and rearview mirrors, Lawson scanned the area, trying to find a better place to wait.

"We gotta be this close. If we try to roll up, it'll give him opportunity. Plus, his hatchback could be filled with who knows what. These meth guys roll around with some dangerous chemicals. Volatile, to say the least. I've got seven mouths to feed at home. I don't need this thing ending with a bang."

Lawson was eager to prove himself to the senior and far more experienced Hicks. This was his chance. In Lawson's mind, the move from Texas to Alaska was the pinnacle of his law enforcement career. It had all changed when Lawson saw the posting in the locker room for an opening on the Fugitive Task Force Unit.

Only one downside. The location.

According to his wife, the move had been nothing but a nightmare. Since arriving in Anchorage, their relationship had been strained, to say the least. This morning's fight was the worst they'd had since arriving. It left him exhausted, frustrated, and considering a transfer back to Texas. It would mean giving up on his dream, although the reality of the situation was different than he'd expected.

He had high hopes when he first joined the US Marshals. TV and movies had glorified the career. Upon his entrance into federal service, Lawson was assigned to judicial security. On the outside it sounded interesting, but he soon realized he was no more than a glorified court bailiff. He'd become hesitant to tell people he was a deputy marshal. They immediately pictured Tommy Lee Jones and would then beg for details about his job. He could see the disappointment when he told them. Being responsible for the safety of the federal court's personnel and its prisoners wasn't as sexy as a fugitive hunter.

Upon arriving in Anchorage, Lawson learned the unit comprised only two marshals. Hicks and his now former partner, who Lawson had replaced. A two-man fugitive recovery unit for a city of four hundred thousand. There were other marshals who worked and supported the task force when needed, but most of the time they worked with the Anchorage Police Department.

It had been slow since he'd arrived and he hadn't made a fugitive recovery case worth talking about, which only furthered the argument by his wife that there was no point in being there. Until this morning when he walked through the doors of their small office to see Hicks. His normal grin stretched to a broad smile.

"Ready to catch your first big fish?"

They'd been staring at the same Volkswagen hatchback for the last forty-five minutes. One of the local patrol officers had called it in after running the tag, only to find the plate was linked to a parole absconder by the name of Walter Grizzly, the proverbial big fish. Grizzly had failed to meet the conditions of his parole after serving a few years on a local meth distribution case that went federal because of the quantity of drugs and lab used to make it. A prisoner reduction program put him on a path to early parole. And it hadn't been long until he'd violated the conditions of his release.

Drugs and violent crime filled the pages of Grizzly's criminal history file. He led a small group of white supremacists known as The Way, who made their money selling crystal methamphetamine. They had a stranglehold on the market and used a heavy hand in controlling their territory. A member received his Mark—a tattooed black *W* with a red triangle pointing up from behind like a mountain top—by committing murder.

HICKS WAS right about Grizzly being a killer. Lawson had read the file. His hand had trembled then, just as it did now. About six years ago, Grizzly killed a guy by the name of Trevor Lively in a poker game, breaking his neck with his bare hands in a fight over a few hundred dollars. The key witness disappeared. Evidence was destroyed or deemed inadmissible due to poor handling. Grizzly walked on the murder. Bold red letters atop Grizzly's file listed him as an ADV—Armed, Dangerous, and Violent—apprehension. Lawson stared at the red letters now. He could not will his hand to stop trembling.

Hicks had earlier put in a call to Anchorage PD and requested SWAT assist in the takedown. Anchorage's tactical operations division was dealing with an evolving barricade situation, which had tapped their resources and manpower. A deranged man had abducted a child off a school bus in broad daylight. There was a citywide manhunt underway and most of the city's units were tasked with assisting.

But Hicks knew the shift commander and was able to finagle two marked patrol units to support himself and Lawson should Grizzly present himself. They were now parked a couple blocks away and given strict orders to stay out of the area until Hicks called for the assist. He didn't want the cruisers to spook their target.

Hicks had nearly twenty years of law enforcement experience on Lawson. He also had a big family. He never tired of telling stories about his chaotic home life, his seven children ranging from the age of three to seventeen, a pair of twins smashed in the middle. But the job never seemed to bother him. Hicks let stress roll off him like water off an umbrella. Even now, as they sat in their Taurus in the pouring rain and sleet, waiting on a killer to show himself, Hicks's face still held the hint of a smile.

They had an Anchorage PD radio in their car to communicate with their local law enforcement counterparts. They were set up on a back channel and the radio had been silent. Lawson sipped his coffee, now lukewarm. Even though the heat was running in the Taurus, he shivered. The cold didn't bother Hicks, and Lawson wondered if he'd adjust to it over time. His misery and loathing of all things Alaskan stopped the minute he saw their target exit a barroom.

Walter Grizzly walked towards his Volkswagen. The roof was held on by bungee cords, and the back hatch looked as though it had been replaced from a salvage part and didn't match the lime green of the other three sides. Lawson was surprised that the bear of a man could fit in the car, and had it not been under such dire circumstances, it might've been comical.

Lawson almost didn't notice the thin, skeleton-like man walking just behind Grizzly as the two made their way to the Volkswagen.

Hicks keyed up the radio from his lap. "Everybody get ready to move. I've got eyes on the target. Grizzly is on the move. Todd Lankowski is with him. He doesn't have an active warrant but consider him armed and dangerous."

Hicks then looked at Lawson. "We cannot let them get in that car. Do you understand me? We do not want them getting mobile."

Lawson didn't think the car looked like it could get very far.

Hicks grabbed the door handle and tossed another glance at Lawson. "You ready?"

Lawson nodded and did the same. He removed the Glock from his thigh holster and drew down on the big man, aiming for the center of his massive chest.

"U.S. Marshals! Put your hands up! Do it now! Walter Grizzly, you are a fugitive from justice, and you are being placed in our custody!" Hicks's voice was loud, firm, and direct, the exact opposite of his easy-going manner.

He was tense, and Lawson heard it. He fought to control the shaking in his hands. This was the first time he'd ever pointed a gun at another person in a true life or death situation.

Grizzly stopped six feet from the passenger side door of the beat-up Volkswagen. He and Lankowski raised their hands up. The thinner man put his hands up higher. Grizzly only brought his up to about the center of his chest, almost as if he were offering more of a shrug than a surrender.

Lankowski, following Grizzly's lead, lowered his hands halfway. His eyes were wild and, even through the distortion of the rain, Lawson could see that he was high on meth. His head moved from side to side and his feet continually shuffled. He was antsy, adding to Lawson's nervousness.

Hicks stepped around the front end of the car and was now near the curb. Lawson came up alongside him, their shoulders nearly touching. Hicks continued delivering commands.

"Get on the ground! Face down! Do it now!"

Lawson kept his gun trained on Grizzly who didn't follow the instructions and remained motionless. Lankowski began to get down, but stopped midway when he saw Grizzly had not.

Sighting down the end of his barrel, Lawson saw the front sight post of his Glock taking on the tremble in his hand. He fought to control the dots' oscillation when he saw something that sent a shiver down his spine. Walter Grizzly smiled.

"Don't do it!" Lawson said. "Don't reach!"

Hicks then started screaming, on a loop, "Get down! Get down!"

Lankowski leapt in front of the Volkswagen's hood, his thin body disappearing.

"Shit!" Hicks yelled as he turned his weapon in the direction of the thin man. "Lankowski's on the move. Stay with the target. Stay with Grizzly."

Lawson had lost sight of Grizzly for a split second and in that time, the large man had brought up a pistol from the small of his back. He fired twice at Hicks before Lawson could return fire.

Hicks yelled as he fell back. Lawson fired, but Grizzly was already on the move. Gunfire erupted.

Lankowski stood up and fired over the roof of the hatchback. Rounds ripped across the Taurus' hood. Lawson ducked and scrambled away from the onslaught of bullets, crawling between the two vehicles. He felt exposed and feared Grizzly would appear and stomp his head into the ground.

Hicks was lying on his back. His hands were pressed on his right side. His eyes were filled with fear as Lawson pulled him away.

"I'm hit!" Hicks's hands were slick with blood. "Bad one. Below the vest." He coughed blood.

Lawson grabbed Hicks by the collar with one hand while he continued to point his weapon in the direction of the threat. He pulled Hicks along the wet asphalt toward the back of the Taurus while firing several rounds of poorly aimed suppressive fire.

Lawson was halfway from the rear of their car when gunfire forced him to release Hicks and dive for cover. Rounds skipped off the street in front of him. Hicks crawled over and settled against the driver's side wheel well. Lawson fired another volley and came up alongside in a low crawl.

"Keep the pressure on it." Lawson took two deep breaths. "I'm going to end this."

A bullet punctured the Taurus's hood only a few inches from the top of Hicks's head. Lawson took up a more stable shooting platform, trying to recall the fundamentals of sight picture and trigger control from his range training. From the prone position, Lawson steadied his gun hand with his left as he scanned for a target.

The gun battle hit a lull, and the area fell silent except for the low gurgle of Hicks choking on his blood.

"Hang in there. The cavalry is coming." Lawson heard the sirens and knew they were close, but the passing seconds felt like hours. Then he saw a bit of Lankowski's shoe sticking out from the front end of the Volkswagen. Lawson fired and his slide locked back. Empty. As he reached for his spare magazine, he heard a scream.

"Make 'em count, kid," Hicks said between raspy wheezes.

A roar like that of a bear temporarily drowned out the sirens. Grizzly rose on the other side. His gun pointed out toward Lawson. He unleashed several shots. Lawson's left bicep felt like it'd been hit by a ninety-mile-an-hour fastball. The next round hit him while he rolled. Adrenaline masked his comprehension. He felt the hot stinging in the meat of his upper right thigh.

The third round of Grizzly's assault found its mark through Lawson's trapezius, a few inches from his neck. Lawson collapsed, unable to move. He looked to Hicks and saw the life fading from him. Hicks said something Lawson couldn't hear and then gave a weak smile before aiming and firing two rounds. The bullets sailed through the air, missing both Grizzly and Lankowski, striking the back end of the Volkswagen.

The next thing Lawson knew, he was airborne, rocked back by a fireball. He landed flat on his back. His head thudded against the hard asphalt. Burning flesh permeated the air. Where was the source? Lawson's body was disconnected from his mind. His vision flickered. Sounds echoed in an endless dark canyon. Slushy snow fell on his blood-covered face. He could no longer feel the tremble in his hand. He could no longer feel his hand. Or anything else.

Blackness encroached from the corners of his eyes. Lawson's last image was of Lankowski's twisted smile, and the shadow cast by the larger man standing behind him.

TWO

HATCH SAT WITH HER BACK AGAINST THE WALL AND LEGS STRETCHED out along the booth in the same restaurant where they'd said goodbye years ago. Being back here now felt odd. She always wondered what it would be like to see Cruise again. The anticipation of seeing his smile, hearing his voice, feeling his touch, left her palms sweaty.

She had met him after first making Task Force Banshee. He was a SEAL, part of an instructional cadre at an amphibious assault course. During her time there in Coronado, the two had proved they were as intense in the bedroom as they were on the battlefield. But the brightest flames burn fastest, and it wasn't long before life and circumstance conspired to snuff it out.

Sitting at the same table where they'd last said goodbye seemed like as fitting a place as any to pick up where they had left off. It was Cruise who alerted Hatch to the Talon Executive Service team that was sent to kill her. If it hadn't been for him and his early morning text message, Hatch doubted she would've been able to circumvent the threat. She owed him a debt of thanks, but beyond that, he owed her the answer to a question burning a hole in the back of her mind since she'd first received the message.

How did Cruise know?

The only person capable of answering walked through the door. It had been five years since Hatch last saw him, but seeing him now, she couldn't tell a day had passed. The tingle in her scar returned. Hatch ran her fingers along the raised puffiness of twisted thorny branches of scar tissue, wrapping her right arm from her wrist to her shoulder.

A wise café owner in Africa had taught her not to be ashamed. He told her not to hide it, to embrace it, which in the time since she'd learned to do. But here now, seeing Cruise again, she was conscious of it and wished she had opted for long sleeves.

Hatch was no longer the person she was when she first entered the military. She wasn't the woman Cruise had known. The IED that tore her arm apart fractured her life, and from that point forward, everything had changed.

Cruise looked as though the battlefield hadn't broken him. In fact, he somehow looked younger, happier. The years between their last encounter had resulted in markedly different impacts, at least on the outside.

He stopped a few feet away, arms crossed over his chest, eyes narrowed, smile on his lips. "Well, if it isn't Rachel Hatch in the flesh."

In the flesh. Even his words stung, but what hurt worse was the way his eyes immediately darted to her arm. When he met her gaze again, he gave her the pity look.

"Don't give me that look."

"It's just—I should've been there for you." His arms dropped and he held his hands out, palms up. The edge on his face faded.

"You were deployed at the time. It didn't matter. Besides, whatever we had ended long before this." Hatch slapped the scar, showing her indifference to him. She didn't know if it worked.

"I think I read somewhere that you had died in a horrible fire."

"I read that, too."

"Well, you look great for a zombie. But I hope you're searching the menu for something to eat."

Hatch felt her cheeks warm, the redness blotching her pale complexion. Cruise smiled. He was a handsome man, but Hatch knew him on a deeper level. Beneath his tough exterior was a kind soul. Cruise had laid it bare one night while having a midnight picnic overlooking the San Diego Bay. They were lying under the stars on the grassy Turner Field on the amphibious Coronado base. On that night, the moon looked as though it rested atop the placid water. It was the first time Hatch told him she loved him. As their lives drifted apart, Hatch promised herself that someday they would meet back where the moon kissed the water.

Cruise left for an eighteen-month deployment just as Hatch had been selected for Task Force Banshee. Even operating in the same theater, it was like living in two different worlds. They'd see each other on random occasions and although the time was passionate, it was brief. They were both married to the military. And now they were both effectively divorced.

Hatch let the thought marinate in her mind as she looked at the man. "Do they still make those coffee cakes? Those oversized ones?" Hatch could almost taste them.

Keeping conversation light, Cruise replied, "They do. I haven't found any better in all my travels." He leaned back in his seat and called over in the direction of the kitchen, "Sherry, two cakes!"

Sherry, a cute dark-haired waitress in her late twenties, approached a moment later with two plates on a tray balanced in one hand and a pot of coffee in the other. She was followed by the scent of cinnamon sugar as it trailed from the coffee cakes. After topping off both mugs with fresh java, she winked and returned to her station.

"How'd you know about Talon?" Hatch asked.

"Wow. I haven't even had my first bite." Cruise set his fork down. He dragged a hand across his stubble and blinked a few times. "Listen, I'm gonna tell you some things and I want you to hear me out to the end."

"I'm listening. I'll eat, you talk." She smiled and cut a fork full of the coffee cake.

"I work for Talon."

Hatch nearly spit the food out of her mouth. She scanned the room for a threat.

"Relax." He attempted to calm her by holding his hands in front of his chest. "That's why I said you have to hear me out. It's just me."

Hatch continued to look around the dining room.

Cruise swept his hand across the table and put it on her right wrist. His pinky finger touched the scar. "It's me, Hatch. Give me one reason you shouldn't trust me."

"How about a dozen of them?"

His smile returned. "Give me five minutes and if you aren't satisfied, I'll wait here while you leave."

She gazed into his eyes for several seconds. She'd seen the man in battle, ready to kill. Remembered the look on his face and the intensity in his eyes. That wasn't there now. She relaxed a little. "I don't understand."

"You've got Talon all wrong. It's not what you think. They are cutting-edge defense contractors. We handle some of the most dangerous missions in the world, and trust me, the guys in my unit are as good as they come."

"Yeah, they're good all right." Hatch felt the rage rise inside her like bitter bile. "Good at hunting down a woman and her family. Tell me, Cruise, are my niece and nephew dangerous threats?"

"What happened to you was an anomaly."

"An anomaly?"

He kept going. "Talon is a private security company, plain and simple. Government contract work, foreign and domestic. What happened to you was done by a rogue element, a couple of old war horses with skeletons in their closets. Ones I guess they were willing to kill to ensure remained hidden."

"My father was one of those old war horses." She grabbed her napkin and wiped her lips.

He reached for her wrist again, this time pulling her toward him. "I know. Listen, that regime is gone. You ended it. Talon wants to set things right after what happened in Hawk's Landing. They came up with an offer I think you'll want to hear."

An offer? She almost choked on her water. "First, why don't you tell me how it is you learned they were coming to get me?"

"Total accident. I was in the process of putting a proposal together, trying to see if I could bring you in. We need a strong, tough female like you on our team."

"What does 'female' have to do with it?"

"Come on, you're smart enough to know. On teams like this, similar to your Task Force Banshee, having a female changes the game, especially when she can operate at your level. That's what I thought our team needed, so I was putting a package together to present you for recruitment."

"I feel like you're talking about a free agent athlete."

"I'm talking about tier one operators. And I only pick the best for my team."

"Then let's hear the pitch." She sipped from her mug. "And please make sure not to leave out the part where your company tried to kill me."

"When I was using our internal system to send my recruitment package, your name was flagged."

"What does flagged mean?"

"It means you were a listed target. Talon has an advanced information system. Once a name is flagged, the intel guys build a digital dossier giving the user access to pretty much every piece of the target's life."

"And that's how you found out your employer had sent people to kill me?" She sawed at her food with the knife, cutting it into small pieces.

"Not at first. I was unable to access the mission file associated with your name. It was beyond my clearance, which is odd because there's very little that is." Cruise took the first bite of his coffee cake before continuing. "I gained access through backdoor channels. At first, I thought somebody had already begun a recruitment process on you."

"Any recruitment effort failed the minute you all tried to kill my family." Steam rose from the cup of coffee in her hand. She thought of the fire that consumed her childhood home and all that she loved with it. A fire Talon had started. One that Hatch had extinguished. And in doing so had faked her own death. Since then, she had been looking over her shoulder for Talon's next hit squad. And now she was now having coffee with one of the enemy. What the hell kind of world had she wound up in?

"Listen, what happened to you was wrong. Nobody currently at Talon endorses what happened. And they weren't a part of it. After I brought it to the attention of my boss, a little house cleaning took place." Cruise set his fork down as he slid his hand across to Hatch's again. This time, his thumb caressed the exposed scar. "Nobody will ever come for you again. I made sure of that."

Hatch knew what cleaning house meant. She looked into Cruise's deep, cobalt eyes. He was telling the truth.

"I'm sorry this happened to you," he said.

"Everything happens for a reason." Had Hatch stayed in Hawk's Landing and settled into a life there, girls like Caitlyn Moss and Angela Rothman would be enslaved or dead by now. The course deviation created by Talon's relentless hunt had ultimately put her in position to honor her code. Help good people and punish those responsible.

"The money's not half bad."

His words jostled her back to the present. "What?"

"Talon pays well."

"I don't need blood money."

"It's not blood money. Everything we do is on the up and up. These are government contracts. Every hit is sanctioned."

"Then somebody must've sanctioned what happened to my family and me."

"They did, and I took care of it. Trust me, that's over." His eyes bore into hers. "Talon wants to call a truce."

Hatch sat back, allowing her hand to slip free of his, ending the gentle caresses. "What if I don't like the terms of the truce?"

"I'm trying to save your life, Hatch."

"So, if I say no, I'm dead?"

"If you don't like the offer, walk away. Nobody on Talon's side will ever come for you. It's that simple."

Hatch absorbed it all. If Talon wasn't looking for her, she could return to her life in Hawk's Landing. She could be with her family. And with Savage. "I'll have to think about it."

"Understandable. My commander would like to meet with you if you're interested."

"When?"

Cruise's cell phone vibrated on the table. He looked at the message and then at Hatch. "How does now sound?"

THREE

"Shooters on the line." Laramie's command rang down across the shooting range's leveled asphalt.

The rangemaster orchestrating the drill was none other than FBI legend and ex-Delta commando, Kyle Laramie. Kyle was one of the founding members of the FBI's elite HRT, or Hostage Rescue Team, the unparalleled tactical element created by ex-special forces operatives.

The two newest members of the team, Laura "Babz" Babiarz and Medina, were present among the seven members evenly spaced across the shooting line. A hushed intensity washed over the group of veteran agents.

Laramie had their attention. "You have twenty seconds to fire eight rounds, four standing, four kneeling. You must complete one combat reload during this course of fire. On the command of 'gun,' you will engage the target in your lane and your lane only. Shooters, on my mark. This is the last course of fire, so make them count."

The years away from his hometown of Evans, Georgia, had done little to diminish his thick southern twang or his habits. A mouthful of sunflower seeds bulged his right cheek, making him look like a chipmunk storing nuts.

The final instructions were followed by silence as each of the seven agents stared out at the CM5 target, a cartoon version of a killer with his gun pointed out from the center of his chest. It was the one most used by the Bureau's state and local counterparts. The rules were simple enough. Keep the bullets inside that area. Of course, simple didn't mean easy.

The cartoon bad guy was sighting down a loaded revolver in his right hand. His left hand was squeezed into a fist positioned in the center of his chest. The top knuckle of the left hand was where Special Agent Laura Babiarz focused. It's where she'd been taking aim since the fifty-round qual course began, and it was peppered with holes from her issued Glock 22 .40 caliber semiautomatic pistol. Her hits were grouped tight, making a golf ball sized hole visible from twice her current distance. She had eight more rounds to prove her nickname, Zero, was a compliment. The operator to her right, a twenty-year veteran of HRT named Teddy Johnson, liked to say that 'zero' was the amount of business a woman had on HRT, but Babz was used to being an underdog. Zero to her meant her sight was dialed in for a perfect shot.

Pushing all thoughts of failure from her mind, Babz controlled her breathing and awaited the final command.

"Gun," Laramie barked. A blast of sunflower shells flew from his mouth like buckshot as the range erupted in a volley of gunfire.

Johnson cursed as he fumbled with his draw. Babiarz blocked him out of her peripheral by focusing on her target. She pressed down on her holster's release button with her left thumb. With one swift movement, she shoved the plastic hood forward and drew her weapon from the level two retention holster clipped to the right side of her hip. As soon as the front sight came into her line of sight, she engaged the trigger with the pad of her index finger, squeezing it and feeling the kick of the Glock against the web of her hand.

Holding steady, she released the tension on the trigger, allowing it to reset before firing again. Babiarz had been trained not to slap the trigger. Her finger, once engaged, didn't come back out of the trigger housing until she was either done or in positional transition. She guided it back and forth, forward progression, then squeezing firmly.

The slide locked to the rear as the last of her four-shot volley left the barrel. Her magazine was empty.

Keeping her weapon pointed at the hairy-knuckled cartoon aggressor, Babiarz dropped to her right knee. She took a moment to re-balance in the kneeling position. She fired using the same fundamentals to keep her aim true.

Train as if it were the real thing. That way when it comes, you've already done it a thousand times before.

Laramie's wisdom looped inside her head.

Babiarz continued to sight down her weapon at the target, canting her wrist inward, her palm toward her face. With her left thumb, Babiarz pressed the mag release. The hard plastic magazine clanged to the ground near her knee. Keeping her eyes on the target and the front sight post in line with the top knuckle, Babiarz grabbed her spare—and final—magazine from her mag carrier.

Without moving her weapon hand or looking at the gun itself, Babiarz maintained her focus on the target while sweeping upward with her offhand containing the replacement magazine. She seated it firmly, feeling it lock into place with a click. Her thumb engaged the slide release. The Glock slide rocked forward, putting it back in battery by chambering a new round. The entire combat reload only took her a matter of seconds.

She squeezed off four more shots, completing her kneeling four-shot component and ending the course of fire. Babiarz scanned the target area, moving her head from left to right before returning to a standing position. This threat scan had been instilled in her by her father and further ingrained by her first range master at Quantico. It was a tactic she still used today.

Harold "Hal" Babiarz handpicked Laramie when HRT was in its inception. The two served in the military together and reconnected when the FBI created a tactical element capable of handling domestic critical incidents with military precision.

Babz had been trying to walk in her father's footsteps ever since he'd pinned the badge to her chest six years ago. The meteoric rise she'd envisioned for herself had been elusive, though. Instead of landing a big field office gig in Boston, New York, or L.A., she had wound up in Denver's satellite office in Lander, Wyoming, covering much of the least populated state in the continental United States. She put in for a transfer to the big time three times, and all three times she'd been denied. Her father had offered to grease the wheels for her. Put in a good word. She'd thought of taking him up on it, but she hadn't yet given into the temptation. The easy road was better left untraveled. Everything she'd achieved, she had earned. It was a source of pride for her, and she had every intention of keeping it that way.

Gunshots from her neighboring agents continued for another several seconds while they finished up their eight-round volley. The last to finish was Johnson, who completed a moment before Laramie called, "Cease fire." Johnson finished the qual the same way he started, with a muttered curse of frustration under his breath. Babz eyed his target and counted seven misses on the outside edges of his paper, five of which had come in the last stage.

The twenty-five-yard distance was challenging for a handgun and was typically the longest shot made during a qualification run. Under stress, the difficulty ratcheted up a hundredfold. Today's qual course proved to be just that for Johnson. Not for Babz, though. Today was just another day on her favorite proving ground.

"Shooters, holster your weapons and make sure your lane is clear," Laramie ordered. "Range is no longer hot. I repeat, the range is no longer hot. Shooters, walk your lane, police up your brass and magazines. After that, head to your targets and stand by."

All agents did as instructed.

Once close to the targets, Babiarz analyzed hers carefully. She was always most critical of herself. All fifty rounds were packed into the same hole, no bigger than a silver dollar, but there was always room for improvement. She realized they could've been tighter. She bit the inside of her lip, a painful quirk and immediate punishment to the disappointment she felt. *Perfect practice makes perfect;* a quote her father stole from Vince Lombardi, floated into her mind. He'd used it on a near constant basis while she was growing up. Now it was part of her own inner monologue.

"Nice grouping, Agent Babiarz," Laramie offered, as he walked by.

In the group setting, Laramie always referred to her in the formal, using her title and last name to address her. She had gotten used to it over the last year since he'd arrived. But if she had her druthers, she preferred the nickname her father had given her. The one she used when introducing herself. Babz.

Laramie made his way over to Johnson's lane. The seasoned range-master marked each missed round with a flick of his marker, annotating the two holes outside of the acceptable target area. "If you missed one more, you'd be reshooting the qual."

"A pass is a pass," Johnson grunted.

"Maybe it'd serve you well if you'd come out here more often or else hang it up. HRT shooters maintain."

"RHIP."

Rank Has Its Privileges.

Laramie shot a glance over at Babz. She pretended not to be eavesdropping. But she caught enough of Laramie's expression to know he was hot. Agents assigned to HRT had a near limitless supply of ammunition and access to ranges to use it. There was no excuse for Johnson's sloppy shots.

"Not in the unit I founded. Rank was earned. The standard never wavers. Want to run it again?" Laramie offered to Johnson.

"Nah, I'm good. Got a hot date." Johnson dusted off his knees and gave Laramie a look. The two had butted heads since Laramie took over the range responsibilities over after Ben Hughes retired. Hughes had let some things slide and allowed range time to become more of a social setting than a training ground.

Laramie took the position at the request of the team commander, Cal Roe. His marching orders were simple. Get HRT back to the gold standard envisioned by its founders. Johnson was not a fan of the change and showed it.

"Your prerogative. I'll document the scores and forward them on. You're free to go." Laramie then turned to the group. "Anybody want to stick around and do some target work? We've got plenty of daylight and rounds to burn."

Babz nodded, but the other operators clustered together and joined Johnson with their grumbled excuses. The idle chatter stopped the moment Roe exited the double-wide range trailer the team used for classes and range admin details. He walked directly over to Laramie. Their exchange occurred outside of earshot and was further obstructed by the collective grumbling. When Roe showed up, it always meant more work, putting everyone in a foul mood. Everyone but Babz. Even from a distance she could read Roe's lips and took a deep breath to prepare her mind for what was coming.

Babz walked over to a canopied row of metal tables and benches. She was already reloading her mags when she heard Johnson snark, "Looks like our rookie hotshot's taking some extra time on the range."

"Maybe that's why she puts all fifty in the hole," Laramie fired back. Satisfied he'd silenced the gruff operator, Laramie called his team to attention. "Commander Roe has something he'd like to share personally."

Laramie stepped aside, giving Roe the floor. Roe stood at a modified parade rest as he waited for silence. When he had it, he got right to the point. "Parker, your request to transfer over to Bravo Team has been approved. Effective immediately, you'll be under Darren Roberts. That means we have an opening for one of our new operators to move up from perimeter to entry team."

Babz looked over at Kevin Medina. His mouth curled into a smile. He gave Babz a playful wink, to which she cracked her knuckles. The two had joined up at the same time and had been facing off from the beginning. If Medina wasn't always pitted against her, Babz could see them being friends. But then she reminded herself he wasn't really her competition. Her only real competition was herself.

Roe's sharp gaze landed on Babz. "Everything in HRT is earned. Time for you to earn your first promotion." He nodded at Laramie, who took over.

"Medina, Babiarz, get a full duty loadout with two spare mags and get back on the line. I hope you're ready, 'cause we're about to do some shooting."

Babz spent a few minutes loading up her mags. Her thumb ached at the effort. The last few rounds were tough to get in place with the resistance offered by the tightly coiled springs. A little extra umph forced each mag to its fifteen-round capacity. She then shoved a mag inside the empty gun and brought the slide forward, chambering a round. She ejected the magazine from the Glock and topped it off again before seating it back into the weapon. Fifteen in the mag and one in the pipe. A full duty load.

Being the first woman to make the FBI's Hostage Rescue Team was the first step. Proving she deserved to stay was next.

Babz walked to the line and prepared her mind for the task ahead.

FOUR

HATCH FOLLOWED CRUISE THROUGH THE DOUBLE DOORS OF TALON Executive Services. On the outside, the building looked like nothing more than a bank or brokerage firm.

As they entered the temperature-controlled lobby, Hatch noticed several well-dressed employees going about their business. To an outsider, it would look no different from any other business office. But Hatch knew all these busy worker bees served a violent endgame. If guys like Cruise were the brawn, then this was the brain.

"Talon has two main branch offices." Cruise explained as he escorted Hatch to the main desk where two well-armed security guards sat. "TES was founded by some of the original team members of Army's Delta Force and Navy's Team Six."

Over the years the names of the elite had changed hands and were still heralded by some as the golden years of special operations. Cruise's reference harkened back to the days of her father. He remained a golden memory, while exposure to the truth had tarnished so many others.

"The rivalries were as big as their egos," Cruise said. "Talon Executive Services' first location was decided by a coin toss."

"If this is one of the main branch offices, then I think it's safe to say

Navy won the toss," Hatch replied, noting they were less than two miles from Naval Amphibious Base, Coronado.

"Twice, actually. The main branch is located near Damn Neck, Virginia. Over the years, as TES grew, we've established satellite offices in almost every state in the country and an equal number spread throughout the world."

"Is this still part of the recruitment package? You sound like you're reading off a brochure."

"We have those too if you'd like to read along." His smile broadened, crinkling his eyes.

Those eyes. How many nights had she lain next to him and watched them drift shut? She felt it again. The warmth in her cheeks, rising from her rapidly beating heart. She choked out a laugh. The camouflage worked.

Cruise continued. "Talon casts a wide net, but we have specialists of the highest caliber."

Hatch thought of the men that had come for her. Now, after being here with Cruise, something about it felt different. She now saw TES for what it is. A government contractor. This was Hatch's world. Rather, the one she'd left behind. She'd been drifting ever since. But here she was being led on a guided tour by the man she had once thought would be the only man in her life.

After the overwhelming realization that Talon wasn't the evil monster she'd believed, came a more terrifying one. "What about the men who came for me in Hawk's Landing?"

"I already told you. We took care of that."

She exhaled in frustration. He'd been offering the same answer, but thus far had provided no proof. "That's not what I'm asking about. The actual hunter-killer team, those were young men, not guys my father's age."

Cruise stopped and faced Hatch. His smile disappeared. There was sadness in his cobalt eyes that wasn't there a moment ago. "You're right about that. I know where you're going with this and I'm warning you, it's a dark place."

Hatch disregarded the warning. *Killing another human being is the most serious of all business.* Her father went on to say. *Each life must be weighed against the plainest of truths. Is the cost of their soul worth the weight added to your own?*

"Did they know why? Did they know the real reason they came after me?"

"No, they didn't." The muscles of his jaw rippled as he averted his gaze.

She felt it now. The weight of it all hit her. They were following orders, like they had been taught since boot camp. Only those giving the orders had placed them in grave danger.

The Army motto, *Mission first, people always,* came to mind. But the often forgotten second part laid the foundation for Hatch's code. People always.

The security guard smiled at Cruise. "Back so soon? I thought your team was on a week of R and R?"

"You know how it is. Bad guys be doing dumb shit." This got a laugh from the guard. "This is my plus one. Tracy should have called ahead on that." Cruise tapped his watchband against a raised pad atop the lacquered oak security desk. A light went from red to green, and a thin shield retracted.

"Pretty cool, huh?" Just like that, Cruise was back. Not a trace of the previous sadness remained. The brightness returned, restoring the blue to the eyes she remembered. "The shield is bulletproof. It can pretty much stop anything, except an RPG."

"Impressive." Hatch walked with Cruise to an elevator waiting area with twin doors. Another gray pad, like the one at the guard desk, was affixed to the wall and evenly spaced between the sets of elevator doors. The right elevator chimed, and the doors opened. "There's no call button. The fob does the work. The left elevator only comes online in an emergency and leads to a fallout shelter below with a multi-staged defense system. Beyond the fallout shelter is a network of tunnel egress points."

"Sounds like a hell of a bugout plan."

"When you kill some of the world's most dangerous people, you've gotta be prepared for all comers." They entered the elevator. The doors closed, sucking all sound and half the air out of the compartment. Cruise lowered his voice. "When we have more time, I'll give you the grand tour."

They stopped at the fourth floor. Cruise led Hatch out.

"Most of the floors are filled with the intel and logistic teams. There's a lot that goes into these kinds of operations. If teams like mine are the fist, this is the heart and soul of it. Fourth floor is ops, secure access only, but you've been granted a visitor's pass."

They moved into a secondary space where Cruise stood for a moment. There was a camera in the corner and a heavy steel door in front of them. Hatch didn't like the confines of the space. If there had been any other motive to Cruise's invite, this would be a bad place to be.

A moment later, a buzz sounded, and the latch on the heavy door released. The door opened and they entered a dark room. Cruise shut the door behind them, and she heard the door latch as it closed. A buzzer sounded, indicating that the lock was secured.

Hatch looked around. Blue light emanating from monitors all around the room served as the only illumination. It looked more like the operation center of an aircraft carrier than an office space. Hatch recognized it immediately. It was a "skiff", short for Sensitive Compartmented Information Facility or SCIF, a self-contained information superhighway used by Intel and special ops around the world where secure communications, transmissions, and operations could be planned.

A man with broad shoulders and close-cropped black hair turned to greet them. Hatch thought of Dalton Savage. And in that same span of time, she felt conflicted as she stood beside Cruise, their bodies close enough that she could feel his warmth.

"Ready to meet the group?"

"Ready as I'll ever be." Hatch nodded. Cruise's voice silenced her inner turmoil. She followed his lead.

"Jordan, this is Rachel Hatch."

"Jordan Tracy." He extended his hand.

Hatch shook Tracy's hand. There was a slight hesitation on her part. Shaking hands with a former enemy took some getting used to. It appeared to have gone unnoticed. "Thanks for extending the offer." She released her grip. "And people usually just call me Hatch."

"Well, Hatch, I sure as hell am glad you took me up on my offer. I knew your father. And for what it's worth—I'm sorry about what happened."

"War is tricky business." She thought of the men she killed in the backyard of her family home. Soldiers sent to kill on the orders of another. The fist not knowing the heart's true intent.

"The past aside, coming to work with us here at Talon will feel like you're back in your old unit. Chris Bennett, your former team commander, gave you a glowing recommendation. Told me he would take you back in a heartbeat, if given the chance."

Hatch thought of her second passage through The Gauntlet. A feat only few could qualify for, and fewer could complete. She had done it twice, the second time after nearly losing her right arm. She'd made peace with Bennett on his decision to deny her reentry to her old unit. They'd cleared the air before Africa, but hearing it again felt good.

"He's telling the truth, Rach."

Rach, Hatch thought. She hadn't been called that in years. She'd forgotten how it sounded coming out of his mouth. The whispered promises all came crashing back. A part of her that had been lost, returned.

"I'm interested in seeing what Talon does," she said.

"I had planned to have us meet later, but something's come up and I thought instead of giving you a boring speech, we'd show you what we do."

"Like a demonstration?" Hatch looked at the other men seated around the briefing table.

"Better. We've just been tasked." Tracy's southern drawl became more pronounced when he smiled. And he had one stretched from ear to ear. "Up for a little road trip?"

"Where to?"

"Ever heard of Breakneck, Alaska?"

Hatch shook her head.

"Well, neither had I, until I got the call. Shit broke bad. And we're going in. Wheels up in thirty. You game?"

Was she? Two worlds collided, and she took a moment to sort them out. Hatch was free and clear. Cruise told her so, and being in this place and meeting Tracy only further confirmed it. She could go home. Back to Hawk's Landing. Back to her mother and niece and nephew, and to Savage.

"They killed a Deputy US Marshal," Tracy said.

Visions of Hawk's Landing faded.

"Shot his partner three times and took him prisoner. We're going in to set things right. Full briefing on the plane. Will you be joining us?" Tracy was already moving toward the door.

Hatch chewed her bottom lip as though she was contemplating the offer, but she had already decided. "Last place I came from was pretty damn hot. Might as well cool off for a bit."

FIVE

BABZ WATCHED LARAMIE GO TO THE TARGET SHED. HE RETURNED looking like a carnival clown, holding strings for seven helium-inflated balloons in each hand. A burst of laughter erupted from the group of men who were grabbing their fifty-round boxes of duty ammo as they headed to the range trailer.

"Look Babz. Laramie brought you a birthday present." It was Johnson who led the chorus of taunts. A big smile formed on his face when several of the others chuckled.

"Maybe you boys should stick around and watch," Laramie challenged. "You might learn something."

Babz walked over and took her half of the balloons. A string connected each to a weighted end. She began dropping the balloons in staggered intervals along her lane of fire leading to her target. Medina did the same. Seven balloons now impeded her line of sight, starting at the twenty-five-yard line with the last one bobbing three feet from the target.

Babz replaced her target, using a stapler to attach it to the wood frame. The target fluttered in the breeze ahead of the eight-foot berm of repurposed rubber chunks that served as a backstop.

"May the best man win!" Medina called over from his lane.

"I hope the best man is a woman."

After her lane was set, Babz walked back to her start point. Instead of starting at the three-yard line, she opted to begin her course of fire from a distance and work her way in. She walked past the twenty-yard mark and stopped at a faded white line marking the thirty-five-yard distance. She closed her eyes, taking a moment to visualize her shots.

"You boys might want to clear back. Looks like Agent Babiarz is going to put in some work." Laramie's boast barely registered as she cleared everything from her mind, just as he'd taught her to do.

"Playing favorites, Laramie?" Johnson called out.

"Let's let the shooting speak for itself," Roe barked.

A hush fell over the range. Babz stood still with her hands relaxed at her sides. She tapped her fingers twice on the textured grip of her pistol, a silent prayer for guidance. Laramie referred to the range as the temple. He said the connection between gun and gunslinger was a spiritual one. Over the time they'd trained together, his words became hers.

This time, there was no command from Laramie. No order to fire. No timeline to meet. This was a skill drill. Laramie gave her a nod, conveying his faith in her. "When you're ready, Agents. The range is yours." He then raised his voice to the group of onlookers. "The range is hot. I repeat, the range is hot!"

Babz began moving in from thirty-five yards out, stepping in a slow, steady progression. She withdrew her gun, keeping the weapon up and sighting down the Trijicon Ruggedized Miniature Reflex sight at the target ahead. She kept her knees slightly bent and her body squared to the threat. Her bent knees enabled her to keep a level shooting platform while moving, avoiding any up and down bobbing by implementing a Groucho walk, a preferred move and shoot technique. *Only move as fast as you can shoot;* Laramie's words again echoed in her head.

"Pay attention, boys. They're on the move." It was the last thing Babz heard as she closed out the world around her.

The wind tossed the helium balloons into a frenzy. The red and yellow spheres passed back and forth in front of the target at uneven intervals. Her first shot came just before she reached the twenty-five-yard line. The round sailed between each of the balloons, striking center mass and hitting the dark outline of the cartoon gunman's top knuckle.

Babz plodded forward, moving past the first balloon, immediately dropping to her knee, and taking two more shots. At the ten-yard line, she launched into a prone position, fired twice, rolled right, and fired two more times before high-crawling forward on padded knees and elbows to the seven. From there, she fired six more rounds from a kneeling position. She stood and exchanged magazines, placing the partially spent mag into her cargo pocket and swapping it for a full fifteen. A tactical reload allowed a shooter to maintain a constant weapon readiness by always keeping a round in the chamber, unlike the combat reload completed during the qual course, which was done when the mag had emptied, and the slide locked back.

Two balloons remained in her line of sight as she moved in from the seven. The wind ripped across the flat expanse of the shooting range, banging the two balloons together and sending them into a frantic churning movement. Babz fired two three-round volleys at the target. A double-tap to the body and one to the head. Repeat. She delivered these last six shots in quick succession. Take the head when the body doesn't fall. The failure drill designed to end threats from bad guys wearing body armor who don't go down with a center mass shot.

Speed and precision drive the drill's purpose and the head makes a significantly harder target, especially when aiming for the tight gap between the eyebrows where her two headshots overlapped.

When Babz finished, she felt the warmth of the Glock's slide against her indexed trigger finger as she guided it back into her holster. Behind her, she heard Laramie clap his hands together.

Laramie approached with a black Sharpie in hand. "Agent Babiarz, how'd we do?"

"Dropped two." She folded her arms across her chest, pressing the Kevlar vest against her breasts. A trickle of sweat traveled down her cheek and came to rest on her jawline.

Laramie ran his finger over the front of the paper and then along the back, silently counting the number of holes and looking for anything outside the target. Finding none, he uncapped his Sharpie and wrote the number fifty in the top right-hand corner. He initialed and dated underneath the notated score before turning to face Babz.

"Agent Babiarz, do you know why you dropped them?"

"I felt the push. Came after the reload."

"You only take the shot you can make. A forced shot becomes a wasted one. You'd better tighten it up. This is HRT." He eyed Medina's perfect shot group, adding insult to injury. He tapped the hole she had made. "Put 'em all in next time."

"Will do." Babz knew Laramie's comments came from a good place. He'd taken the change of assignment as a stepping-stone to civilian life. His timing couldn't have been better. Since his arrival, he'd been running drills with Babz for the last month and a half. The others were unaware Laramie was the one who'd prepared Babz for HRT. He'd run her through this drill before, so she'd be prepared for anything. She let him down, though he'd never say.

She determined to never let him down again.

Knowing the promotion would go to Medina, Babz walked over to the ammo station and began reloading her magazines. There was nothing to do now but practice. As she walked back to top off her magazines and reface her target for another round of drills, a black oversized SUV with heavily tinted windows pulled up to a stop. Babz recognized the woman's almost imperceptible silhouette before the door opened.

Special Agent Brett Larson exited the vehicle. The senior agent and head intelligence officer assigned to the HRT nodded to Laramie as she strode across the backend of the shooting lanes with Roe in her sights. Laramie returned the nod and gave a tip of his bright red rangemaster ball cap.

Larson did not stop to talk with the other five operators standing around Medina, giving the newest addition to Alpha's entry team a ball busting. She had a thin manilla file folder tucked under her arm as she walked, keeping her hands free to fire off a text or email on her cell phone. She was always communicating with somebody, updating her bosses. Larson paused for a moment under the awning at the picnic table that was littered with boxes of ammunition and ammo cans containing the spent brass policed from the range.

Babz set down the box of training rounds she'd been working on.

Larson surveyed the range. She raised an eyebrow at the balloons scattered about. Her face hovered between amusement and displeasure. "What's going on here?"

"Medina and I went head-to-head for the opening on Alpha team."

Larson glanced to where Medina and his pals were celebrating. The results were obvious enough for her to interpret. Her cool brown eyes settled back on Babz. "You really looking to get ahead and shut the boys' club up for good? Work a big case, show them you've got it upstairs as well as in that trigger finger of yours."

"These *fingers* weren't meant for a keyboard." Babz held up her two trigger fingers. She was an ambidextrous shooter.

"It looks like you're going to get to prove it." Larson tapped the file under her arm. "Remember to think as fast as you shoot." Larson winked as she pushed past and continued to Roe.

Babz watched as the two walked away to the trailer.

Roe called over his shoulder, "Briefing in five."

SIX

THE SMALL TEAM OF TALON OPERATORS USED THE THIRTY-MINUTE window to grab their mission loadout. No weapons or gear were provided to Hatch. Tracy made it clear she was to be an observer only. Cruise had outfitted Hatch with an insulated jacket rated for long term exposure, as well as gloves, a hat, and thermals. They'd made it to Lindberg Field, San Diego International Airport in just under twenty minutes.

What an hour it had been. Hatch was sitting on a Gulfstream 6700 private jet with a team of contractors from an agency who'd tried to kill her only months before. Now, she was bound for Alaska. *Cold day in hell* came to mind.

The Gulfstream was unlike anything Hatch had ever flown in before. It was a functional aerial command center divided into four compartments, not including the cockpit. It was built to house as many as nineteen passengers. Each chair fully reclined, and there were three couches. One of which Hatch and Cruise now shared. It hardly felt like flying.

She ran her hand over the soft leather of the seat. It was smooth, unlike the marred flesh of the hand touching it. Cruise's elbow touched hers. Even though the temperature onboard the aircraft was comfortable, Hatch slipped the jacket on.

"If you want, I can adjust the temp," Cruise offered.

"Not necessary. I'm fine with the jacket." Hatch lied. She was mad at herself for feeling the compulsion to cover her scars when around Cruise.

"Now that we're settled in, I'd like to formally introduce Hatch. As you know, she'll be joining us as an observer on this op with the hopes of piquing her interest enough for her to join this ragtag band of misfit children." Jordan sat across from the rest of the team and pressed a button on a table next to him. A thin forty-inch LG 4K ultra-high-definition flatscreen arose, blocking two of the windows. "Cruise, would you like to do the introductions?"

Cruise gave a bow. "Let's see...why don't we start with the elephant in the room?"

"Funny. I always considered myself more of a rhino," the man seated in the chair to the right of Cruise said with a laugh. "I'm Eric Hertzog. But people call me Miles."

"He'd like to think it's because he's smooth like Miles Davis." The man, right of Hertzog said, laughing at his joke before he finished saying it. "But the reality is, we call him that because he's a damn doppelganger for Michael Clarke Duncan from The Green Mile."

Hertzog laughed along with the ribbing. His dark skin gave way to a bright, toothy smile. He reminded her of Dubaku, the big Kenyan who preferred to be called Duke and the man who, in a selfless act, traded his life for hers.

"You're just mad because you hate yours. Ginger here has been begging for a new nickname since he came on board. But if the shoe fits." Hertzog mussed the man's bright red hair and gave a playful shove, nearly knocking him out of his seat.

"I'm Brad Taylor." Ginger gave a wave.

Hatch returned their smiles and was happy to see she wasn't the only one who turned fire engine red when embarrassed. "Strange to say, but it feels good to be here. Thanks for the invite."

"With that out of the way, let's get up to speed on things." Tracy tapped a stylus pen to a digital pad and the LG monitor came to life. A moment later, the black-and-white image of a row of cars along a street came into view. She saw a liquor store and pawnshop. There was a third business on the furthest left of the frame. From the neon beer bottle sign in the window, Hatch assumed it was a bar. She also noticed two men sitting in a light gray Ford Taurus.

"This video is from an ATM across the street from this morning's incident. Not the best quality, but you still get a clear view of what happened. You'll see a large man come into view once I hit play. His name is Walter Grizzly. Belongs to a local white supremacist gang known as The Way. He's accompanied by his scrawny accomplice, Todd Lankowski. These bastards have a reckoning coming, and it's coming at our hands." The southern drawl had crept in again. Not as much as before. Tracy's face was no longer friendly. He was all business now.

"Grizzly and Lankowski got in a shootout with two Deputy U.S. Marshals assigned to Anchorage's Fugitive Recovery Task Force. One of the marshals, Clyde Hicks, was killed on scene. The other marshal was shot several times. Gunfire ignited the backend of the target's Volkswagen, which subsequently exploded. What at first was believed to be a bomb was later deemed a mobile meth lab. The second deputy, Darren Lawson, was taken hostage by Grizzly and Lankowski. The explosion disoriented responding units. Grizzly and Lankowski escaped in the marshal's Taurus."

All eyes were trained on the footage.

"The two men in that Taurus are Hicks and Lawson. Hicks is in the driver's seat." Tracy tapped the tip of the stylus against the tablet's screen. The clock at the bottom of the screen began ticking by.

The video had no audio as it replayed the event. It was like watching a silent western. The Taurus was stopped behind a two-tone Volkswagen hatchback. The two marshals exited their Taurus as Grizzly and Lankowski came into view from the left side of the screen. There was a brief standoff. Even without the sound, Hatch felt the intensity of the moment as the lawmen drew down.

Grizzly and Lankowski raised their hands as the two marshals moved in for the takedown.

"Do you see that? The big guy's actually smiling." Hatch stared at the giant on the screen.

"That's what makes the next part worse," Tracy said.

All hell broke loose a moment later. The gunfire initiated with Lankowski, giving Grizzly an opportunity. Grizzly aimed carefully, shooting Hicks while Lankowski fired wildly, drawing return shots from Lawson who took cover between cars.

Hatch watched as one marshal went to rescue his downed partner dragging him to safety before being shot himself.

Tracy paused the video with a tap of his pen. "Best we can tell from the video, Lawson was shot three times. One in the leg. Two in the torso." Tracy hit play and the video continued.

Lawson was lying face down. Hicks, critically wounded, began crawling toward his partner. He fired a quick burst in the direction of the Volkswagen. Grizzly and Lankowski were already working along the sidewalk in a flanking maneuver. A white flash on the screen blotted the image for several seconds before the camera came back into focus. The footage then showed Grizzly and Lankowski dragging the wounded Lawson away and stuffing him in the back seat of the marshal's own vehicle. Two Anchorage PD marked units rolled up on scene, passing the Taurus as it disappeared off camera, leaving the corpse of Clyde Hicks to burn in the street.

"What's the plan?" Hatch asked.

"Working the problem now. I'll have something together in a couple hours." Tracy tapped his pad and the screen went blank. One press of a button later and the monitor retracted. "We've got about six hours until we touch down in Anchorage. Op briefing will be done once we hit the ground. It may be a while until the next time you get to close your eyes. Everybody power down for a few and get some sleep."

"C'mon Dad, but you promised I could watch TV." Hertzog clasped his large hands together.

Tracy chuckled at the big man and then tapped Cruise. "Meet me in the office for a minute. I want to pick your brain on something."

Cruise got up and carried with him the smell of the ocean. It returned like the waves he surfed, as he leaned back in toward Hatch.

For a second, she thought he was going in for a kiss. Her thought was dashed the minute he grabbed his notepad he'd left behind on the armrest where they'd been sitting.

Cruise looked at her with those cobalt eyes. No smile to make them shine. Cold as steel. "I'll tell you one thing, Rach. They're going to pay for what they did today."

SEVEN

"I WANT TO SEE CLEAR LANES OF FIRE AND CONTROLLED BURSTS. I WANT to see what we pride ourselves on here as members of the Hostage Rescue Team. We are the FBI's elite. There's SWAT, and then there's us. We are the gold standard. This mission is critical because we're bringing back one of our brothers. There's no alternative to what our purpose is today, *gentlemen*. Let me make that clear."

Babz noticed that Cal Roe emphasized the gentlemen when he looked at her. Hoop, as he was known among the team—thanks to his All-American basketball star status during his four years at West Point —had been one of the founding members of HRT. The ex-Delta Force commander was now HRT commander. His hands-on policy ensured that he was present for every mission possible. It was his way of shoving it to the FBI's age standard. He might not be allowed to carry a firearm as a member of the FBI, but they allowed him to remain on as a tactical advisor.

The team viewed Hoop as their true commander. Even Bill Sykes tipped his hat to Hoop when he entered a room, and when Hoop entered the room, he dominated it.

Hoop was nearly a foot taller than Babz, and just about six inches taller than every other man on the team. To say he wasn't thrilled when a female had made HRT would've been an understatement. Hoop's dislike of Babz was predestined. He'd worked with her father back in the day. Hal Babiarz had been a legend among the HRT and was also a founding member. He and Hoop were rumored to have had a long-standing feud. One that Babz felt still hadn't ended. And she was paying the price.

Babz couldn't help thinking contempt for her father was the real reason for Hoop's overt efforts to dismiss any accomplishments she made. Whether it was selection to the team itself or her prowess on the range in their tactical evolutions, anything she did well seemed to only infuriate Hoop further. It was a never-ending cycle of do better, get shamed more.

Hoop's voice boomed through the room. "I'm going to let Sykes run you through the op. Run it tight. Run it like it's the real thing because in a matter of hours, it very well could be."

Bill Sykes was of average height and frame, but he carried himself well with the confidence of a man with experience, and experience he had. He had served in the military before coming to the FBI. Since being on the team, he'd earned the rank of commander. More importantly to Babz, he didn't have a hard-on for her to fail.

Sykes stepped up. "To the two newbies, welcome to the show."

The two shots that had bested Babz on the range evaluation had landed Medina the last slot on the assault team. Always the good sport, Medina gave her a nudge as Sykes recognized them. The smile playing on the corner of his lips put her at ease. Some of the guys would want to win just to beat Babz. Not Medina. He wanted the position. He earned it.

"Right now, due to a higher level than I can speak to, we have another team working a separate angle to bring this mission to resolution quickly. If effective, they'll be bringing our brother law enforcement officer home. We will be prepared to act on our assault plan should theirs fail."

Dan O'Hara put his hand up. He didn't do it sheepishly. These were all tested men, all accomplished operators before becoming a member of the HRT. Many served in the military, or local SWAT departments—some in the largest and most population-dense cities in the country—before making the jump over to FBI and then to HRT. There were thousands of hours of training and hundreds of operations behind the belts of these men. They'd been battle-tested like few had. There was no timidness among the group.

"O'Hara? Something to say, like always?" Sykes cast his eyes at him but softened the question with a half-smile.

O'Hara made a show of lowering his hand. "I just gotta wonder, who gets tapped ahead of us to run an op like this?"

"Like I said, that is above my pay grade." Sykes avoided the answer, something Babz hadn't seen him do in her short time on the team. Her interest was piqued. "This goes above me," Sykes continued. "This goes above Hoop, but we still have to be ready. Murphy's a bastard and he's always out there."

Murphy's Law, every operator's enemy.

Sykes pointed to the large dry erase board. "Only thing you need to worry about right now is committing the grease board to memory."

The eight-by-six board held a diagram of a crudely drawn rectangle representing the structure. The bottom was labeled Front Door and marked with the number one. The remaining three sides continued the numbering sequence counterclockwise from the main entrance.

There was a line dividing the room and there were six black X's scattered around in various positions, representing the hostage takers, plus a circle with a red X in the center of them all. The word, "Lawson," was scribbled alongside it. In a small chart was a list of the members of The Way, the Aryan Brotherhood group.

"Expect every single one of these guys to be armed. They make their money selling meth and my guess is many of them are using, so you're going to be dealing with unstable minds, wild bodies, and unexpected reactions to gunshots should we hit them. Be prepared for anything. We engage our targets if they present a threat, and we do not stop engaging until the threat is down. Is that clear?"

Everybody agreed in unison.

"They've taken over a facility called Camp Hope located near the small town of Breakneck. And when I say small, I mean *small*. Last census had it at one-hundred-thirty souls. State Police are holding tight in the town and using a drone to monitor the perimeter. The terrain is unforgiving. This campground is just south of a glacier. The longer they think we don't know their location, the better."

"Nobody noticed these guys squatting before now?" O'Hara asked. "And how is nobody in this room asking the million-dollar question—who the hell names a town Breakneck?" O'Hara laughed at his own joke.

"First, it's the closed for years. Intel said the gang started using it as their clubhouse a few months back. As for the town's name, well that came about when the founder fell into a crevasse and died. Anybody wanna guess how? Mind your steps out there. You fall into a crevasse, it could be a very long time before your body is recovered, if ever."

"Sounds like a great place for a camp." Medina chuckled under his breath.

Babz smiled.

"Focus." Sykes lowered his gaze at the two of them. "They've converted the camp's cafeteria into a meth lab. That's where we are getting the highest heat signatures. It's a small set-up at forty-by-sixty feet. Been used to house about twenty-five campers at max capacity. It's one of those escape to nature camps. Expect comms to be spotty. The camp is just shy of 6,900 feet elevation. Take the elevation into account when moving. Conserve where you can. Most of the trek in will be on foot."

Sykes then brought up a satellite image. "We don't want a repeat of what happened during the original takedown. A full-sized lab is going to pack a much bigger punch than that Volkswagen did so extreme caution will have to be used. Our original plan was to hit the front with flashbangs. This is still a go, but we are going to bang on the outside for distraction. The two front doors on number one side leave the most exposure should they try to exit that way. We don't want them coming out the front, so we're going to continue to bang that side with our forty-millimeter launchers. I want two members of the team to lay down a heavy layer of tear gas, forcing them out the other two exit points."

Babz soaked it in, memorizing the diagram and plan.

"We have exits on sides two and three. Back of the kitchen is number three side. A small door used for kitchen staff on number two side. These are tighter exit points, which means should they rabbit, we have a better chance of controlling the flow and number of people coming out at any one time, limiting our exposure to gunfire. But let me remind you, the only gunfire I want coming out of that house is from the muzzles of your weapons should they present a threat. Is that clear?"

"Crystal," the group choral.

"A mockup of this layout is set up in hangar bay number two just next door to us. Run it by the numbers until this thing is present in your sleep; until you see the movements in the entry every time you blink your eyes. This has gotta be muscle memory. We must be perfect. Babz, I know you're hanging back on this one, but I want you to get a rotation in with assault team one. Assault team one, when we deploy and move in, you're going to stack up on the number two side. Assault team two, you're going to move your way around to the back, stack up on the door on the three side.

"Murphy, Dunn, you're going to rock the front of that building like a hurricane. Do you understand me? You're going to hit them with flashbangs and then deploy the launchers and draw. The bangs should bring them forward, thinking that we're coming through on a frontal assault. That should give assault team one and two time to get to their entry points. You're going to initiate entry on the first bang. By the second bang, the rest of you better be in and clearing that room. Is that clear?"

"Crystal." This time with a little more gusto. The energy of Sykes was contagious, as was his mission preparedness. It was a clean plan. Clean was good. Overcomplicated plans got people killed.

Keep it simple stupid, and practice 'til it's perfect. Her father had said that to Babz a thousand times when she was a kid and then when she was a cop. Hearing them in her mind now made her feel like he was there with her.

"We've got two birds ready to take us in, should we get the call. Remember, if we're given the green light, it's going to take forty-five minutes under the best of conditions to get from Anchorage to the LZ in Breakneck."

Babz's momentary reprieve evaporated as Hoop walked past her. "Time to prove up, Buttercup."

Medina leaned in. "I don't know if he's talking to you or me."

Babz laughed as she grabbed her gear and headed to hangar two, glad that for once, she and Medina were on the same team.

EIGHT

HATCH AWOKE AS THE GULFSTREAM SLOWED AND DESCENDED, AND THE ride got a little bumpy. She'd slept most of the flight. She looked out the window. Dark storm clouds choked the moonlight as hard rain pelted the plane's exterior and streamed along the window. The lights on the wing reflected off the wisps of clouds they raced through.

Cruise sat across from her and was jotting something into a digital tablet. Without looking up, he spoke in a whisper. "Been a long time since I've fallen asleep next to you."

"I hope you weren't drawing me while I slept." Hatch referenced their favorite movie, Titanic. They'd watched it together at an old movie house after grabbing a couple tacos and Tecates from a food truck. That memory hadn't come to her in a very long time. Its return felt conflictingly good, the warmth of which spread across her body.

"I'm no Jack Dawson but take a look." Cruise remembered that night, too. He turned the pad to Hatch. On it was a mission plan tactical diagram for their three-man assault team. "What do you think?"

"What happened?" Hatch studied the diagram.

"They eluded law enforcement. Anchorage's Gang Task force had information that The Way use a camp in Breakneck as a meth lab."

Cruise tapped the pen and the hand drawn tactical plan dissolved into an aerial map of an ice-covered glacier. She could make out a few structures. "Welcome to Camp Hope. This is a live feed from a drone the FBI sent up. We're patched in."

"Any movement down there?"

"We've visually identified six. Buck Mathers, Sam Kirkland, Frank Winslow, Todd Lankowski, Chris MacIntosh, and our guest of honor, Walter Grizzly." Cruise flicked through a series of still shot images capturing the men named. Hatch committed them to memory.

"Any sign of Lawson?"

"No. This place was designed to be one of those escape-to-nature camps; leave everything behind. No cell reception, nothing. It had been abandoned for years, but it wasn't until a few months ago that Grizzly and his crew started using it as their clubhouse for misfit rejects. The camp's cafeteria has been converted into a meth lab. That's where we believe Lawson is. It'll be our target location. I'd prefer to do a couple of run throughs first but it's a simple smash and grab. Plus, clock is ticking on Lawson if it hasn't already expired."

"The op is a go? You guys are taking the lead on this?"

"Still on standby for now."

"No, we're not." Tracy opened the door to his stateroom and joined them. "The order just came through."

"If this is a hostage crisis of this magnitude, how come local SWAT aren't handling the call?" Hatch asked. "Why call a government contractor when you could deploy the FBI's Hostage Rescue Team?"

"You ever have one of those days where everything that could go wrong did?" Tracy asked.

"More than I care to admit," Hatch replied.

"Well, this is the mother of all days. Locals, with federal support, are handling a child abduction that turned into an armed barricade. The other factor is resources. Anchorage can't deploy units two hours south. Especially with all the recent seismic activity." Tracy scanned his team. "And HRT has been called up. Just got off the phone with my good friend Cal Roe, team commander. He's just been informed through his chain of command that his team will serve as back up. He called me to... express his frustration." Tracy's smile returned and with it his accent. "To put it bluntly. He was downright pissed. But he'll get over it."

The Gulfstream bucked as it descended another hundred feet or so.

"I still don't understand how a government contractor can supersede a federal agency unless—" Hatch let the words trail off while her brain connected the final dot. "Because you *are* a federal agency. But why the smoke and mirrors? Why present yourself as something you're not?"

"Subterfuge," Tracy said. "It allows us a broader scope access point nationally and internationally. It also allows us to be the big bad contractors when things break bad. To the public and pretty much everybody else, we exist but don't exist. Just like your Task Force Banshee. There's no record of it even existing on any of your military records. Sure, there're breadcrumbs, but only if you know what to look for."

"What makes this incident worse than the one with the child taking place in Anchorage?" Hatch said. "Sounds like that's pretty volatile."

Tracy took a moment to compose his answer. "I'd like nothing more than to save every man, woman, and child. But the reality and the ability are far out of touch. What I can do is handle the task I'm given and deliver results with unprecedented precision."

"I think you misunderstood me. I was asking what factors put Talon on the call list?"

"Exposure. The federal government can't handle another Waco. It would bring the country to its knees."

"How do Talon's methods make them better than a team like HRT? That team is chock full of former members of the spec ops community. This is going to sound bad, but what makes you guys any better?"

Hertzog joined the group and theatrically feigned taking an arrow to the heart. Taylor shadowed him. It provided Tracy a chance to redirect.

"Right now, there's one heat signature that hasn't moved," Tracy said. "It's in the center of that room. We believe that's Lawson, and he is still alive. This one will be a full erasure."

"What's an erasure?" Hatch thought of the briefing like this that must have been conducted before coming to the backwoods of her childhood home.

"Basically, we go in, and after the mission is complete, we erase any trace we were ever there."

Hatch couldn't believe what she was hearing. "You're talking about military black ops on US soil."

"It happens every day." Tracy offered a shake of his head. "The world doesn't see it. Because we don't let them."

"If we ever wanted to retire, we could take Vegas by storm with our magic act." Cruise laughed as he zipped up the side of his combat boots.

Hatch thought about her own life and the way her past had been rewritten.

"Your show, your briefing." Tracy took a seat beside Hatch.

Cruise brought the hand drawn digital sketch up on his tablet. "Here's the plan. We've got two front doors here and a front side porch. We've got an outhouse to the right, and as we work our way around on the right-hand side, there's a side entrance. And then, in the back with a kitchen that has now been converted into a meth lab, there is another entrance. Two doors in the front, one on the side, one in the back. Four ingress and egress points. We are going to use two of them, and we'll capitalize on the third."

Using the digital pad, he drew a sloppy version of what he had just described. His wraparound porch was fully drawn, and he scattered some trees around further out and marked in a box "OH," for outhouse. "This is the proximity going around twenty meters or so outside of the cafeteria. This is what we're working with. No trees to provide cover. The outhouse is the only thing close. Further down are the cabins."

Cruise transitioned the image to the live feed, as he had done with Hatch. "This is a glacier, so the going won't be easy. The Suburban we'll use can't make it over the ice. Plus, it would be impossible to mask the noise of a vehicle that heavy crunching ice. There is one road in and one road out of the camp. Two miles from the main entrance is an ATV trail that breaks off to the right. Here." Cruise scrolled the image down. The mud trail branched out from the main road. "The ATV trail leads several miles north to the base of the glacier. We're going to make the trek in on foot from there. Once we cross this icy ridge, it flattens. The camp is in the center. We walk in, hit 'em and forget 'em, then walk back out."

"More like skate back out," Hatch said.

"Not with these babies." Cruise pushed out his boot. To Hatch, they looked like any other cold weather boot. Cruise then pressed a button on the side. A metallic click sounded, and six steel claws popped out from the sole, four equally spaced on either side. The other two were centered, with one being positioned near the toe and the other near the boot's heel.

"Retractable crampons?"

"Yup. Ginger got the idea from those Heely shoes his kids wear. Had our design team build them to spec for an op a while back. They work like magic. They're lightweight and grip the ice. Each claw is a bunch of thin blades close together. They cut into the ice like a warm knife through butter. The blades make lifting the foot easy. But the best, no crunching. These boots enable us to move whisper quiet across the ice."

"We spare no expense here at Talon." Tracy chimed in. "Not trying to be used-car-salesman pushy, but I brought you along so you could see what we do. These boots are but the tip of the iceberg when it comes to the technology and weaponry at our disposal. If you can dream it, our research and design team can make it."

"Impressive."

"Just wait until we hit the ground."

"You talked about erasure. All I'm seeing is an assault plan. Am I missing something?"

Cruise tapped his screen. His diagram drawing came to life.

The animated sketch identified each of Cruise's team dots on the screen by the first initial of their last name. Cruise and Taylor would enter through the side door while Hertzog entered the rear. Dynamic entry with multiple entry points. Overwhelming force with precision execution. Bread and butter close quarters combat stuff. A walk in the park for guys like Cruise and his team. Hatch had no problem with the plan itself. She would have planned something similar. It was what the team did after the diagram show that caught her attention.

"Am I reading that op plan correctly? You're using explosives?" Hatch stared at the words burn it down, written in Cruise's sloppy handwriting.

"We're gonna make a little boom boom with these." Hertzog opened his rucksack that looked more like a fanny pack in his gargantuan hands. Inside were a bunch of grenades. She recognized the M34 White Phosphorus Smoke Grenade. Her father had several. He kept them more as memorabilia than anything else.

"Why are you using Willie Pete on your way out?"

"Like you said, we're going to *burn 'em all*. And that is the candle." Cruise smiled.

"I still don't understand why you'd use a Vietnam era grenade to do the job."

"Talon doesn't only handle the operation. We handle the complete show." Tracy sipped hot coffee while he spoke. "And the biggest beast to control is the media. We've been able to operate with such anonymity for so long because of our ability to do just that."

"What's the spin with the M34s?"

Cruise did his best impression of a news anchor. "The headlines will tell of a group of unstable white supremacist meth pushers who holed up in an abandoned campground with a cache of weapons dating back to Vietnam. A gun battle erupted between the members of the gang during which an old satchel of smoke grenades exploded, killing all but one. FBI's HRT arrived shortly after to find Deputy Marshal Lawson was the sole survivor, saved by an overturned table which shielded him from the blast."

"Remind me to have you write my obituary," Ginger snarked.

"Thoughts or questions?" Tracy asked more to Hatch than anybody else in the room.

"I definitely see why Talon operates under the radar."

"We help people in trouble. And we deliver swift justice on the way out."

"Problem with swift justice, what happens when you get it wrong?" Hatch thought of herself.

"I know you're still raw about what happened to you. I know I sure as hell would be." Tracy laid his accent on thick. "But do you see anything about this group of douchebags that warrant a second thought? The Way's motto is 'Follow me or die.'"

"I'm just saying. Make sure you measure twice, cut once," Hatch said.

"I'm glad you mentioned that. There's one member, a Christopher MacIntosh, who's new. Only been with them for a couple weeks. His parole officer is meeting us in Breakneck and I want you to talk to him."

"Why's that?"

"Because I want you to find out why a former Marine is mixed up with a bunch of neo-Nazi shitheads."

NINE

THE MOON WAS INTERMITTENTLY HIDDEN BEHIND A THIN VEIL OF WISPY gray clouds, leading a wall of dark thunderheads. Moonbeams danced across ice as sleet worked to douse their brilliance. In his haze, it felt as though he was in a dream. The reality of his circumstance wouldn't release him to the dream. It was literally slapping Lawson in the face. Lankowski's steel belt buckle banged into the side of Lawson's face every couple of steps, stinging his already burned flesh.

He could make out footsteps on either side of him. They'd come in faint at first like the rustling of leaves, but as his vision returned, so did his ability to hear. Although he couldn't feel anything below the neckline, he knew he was being carried by the way his head bobbed above the icy snow. He strained to look up, but the pain was too intense.

Lawson's hot breath melted the flakes falling in front of him. A glimmering sheen of ice now coated his face. He was jostled and his head banged loosely, the bridge of his nose bumping into his shoulder and snapping free a bloody icicle that hung from his left nostril.

Fresh blood began working to create its replacement stalactite of blood-covered snot. The cold air gripped his throat and stung his lungs. As odd as the thought was under such circumstances, he decided he hated the cold. And he hated Alaska. He decided right then and there, if he managed to survive whatever this was, that he'd take his wife and unborn child back home to Texas.

Lawson's tolerance for the cold wet embrace of mother nature was worsened by the company he currently kept. He couldn't move his arms or legs. Through his neck, he could feel the tugging motion of his body.

His recall came in small, confusing chunks. Most of which were out of order. The cold air helped jostle his memory. He tried again to piece it together.

Hicks got a tip. A neo-Nazi skinhead named Grizzly had a warrant. ADV. Armed, Dangerous, and Violent. The gunfight flashed back. Lawson could feel the three bullets hit his body. One in the left arm. One in the right leg. One below the neck. He couldn't feel the wounds anymore. Then, Hicks returned fire. Then the flash. How long had he been out?

He willed himself to move, focused on his hands, his feet, but nothing happened. It was like the connection between his mind and body had been severed.

The wind washed out much of what the two men were saying, but he caught bits of the conversation above the gusts.

"How much do you think this guy weighs?" Lankowski said.

"He's dead weight," the other guy grumbled. "Are you sure he's gonna be there?"

"Of course, he's gonna be there. You think a guy like Grizz is gonna sit out? Nah, he wants to get his hands in on this. He's gonna have a little talk with our friend here."

Lawson felt a tug as the man wearing the belt buckle stopped in his tracks.

"Why is it you're so interested in seeing Grizz?"

"Because I earned my place to be here, and I don't want to be out just doing bitch work. I'm ready to prove up. I'm ready to be a member. I'm ready for my Mark."

Lawson felt their stares boring into him.

"Well, Grizz is really careful about who he meets, vetted or not." Lankowski shifted. "Just because you did some hero shit in prison and saved Winslow's ass doesn't mean you get a free pass to join up with us. You can't just run on up there and expect to get to see the King. You know how it works. You gotta earn your keep, just like me."

"I think I proved I can be trusted." The man spat and it hit Lawson on the face.

"Everybody knows what you did in there. That's not what I'm saying, but Grizz is smart. He likes to see things for himself. Plus, nobody here saw you do it. I mean, a few days after you show up, he's got marshals coming at him. He might have questions for you."

"You think I did those extra years in Spring Creek to cop a deal?"

Lankowski chuckled. "You only did five years on a murder rap."

"Murder looks different on the inside of those walls. So does time. And I did both, and that's how I ended up here. I had nothing to do with whatever that shit-show was in Anchorage. I didn't have anything to do with this law dog here. And if you question me on that again, this won't be the only body I drag up this hill tonight."

"Easy man, I was just saying is all. And what makes you think you should earn your Mark before me? I've been with Grizz and the boys a lot longer than you. Going on three months. You ain't been 'round but a minute."

"Time don't mean shit. You know the things I had to do to survive in Spring Creek?" The only answer came in the form of a wind gust that cut across the ice like a scythe. "Didn't think so. I may not have been here. But I've been with The Way for the past five years."

"Inside ain't the same as out?"

"True. Inside you'd already be dead. Talk to me the way you just did again, and you will be."

Lankowski cleared his throat and offered a strained chuckle. "Well, this pig's half dead anyway. You wouldn't have to do much but flick him. Hell, I'm surprised he survived this long. Just look at him."

There was an awkward silence before the men started moving again. Lawson could feel that the lion's share of the load was being carried by the man on his left.

A few feet from the door, Lankowski slipped. His foot shot out from under him, and his body upended, like a poorly placed Charlie Brown kick after Lucy yanked the football away.

Lawson slammed down into the icy ground with devastating force. The searing pain caused a flicker of darkness followed by stars. He fought to remain conscious, afraid the next blackout would be his last.

"Get up on your damn feet. Dumbass!" The man on the left hissed above the wind.

They pulled Lawson off the ground. The snow and ice where his face impacted was now covered in his blood. Fresh droplets added to it as it continued to leak from his damaged face.

They dragged him the last few steps across the glassy surface. The light above the door bathed the belt buckle hovering near his face in a yellow glow. Lawson stared at the silver cowboy, waving his hat atop a bucking bronco. The embossed figure was now outlined in Lawson's blood.

The door swung open. Grizzly's massive form eclipsed the light trying to squeak by.

At six-foot-nine, three-hundred-and-eighty pounds, Grizzly was a behemoth who looked more beast than human. A thin layer of fat insulated bulging muscles. Even in the bitter cold, Grizz stood there wearing a sleeveless hooded black sweatshirt. He looked like a cross between Bill Belichick and Rumblebuffin, the fabled giant from The Chronicles of Narnia. Tattoos covered his exposed skin, disappearing under his thick red beard. Grizz's head was shaved smooth. A solitary red triangle with a thick black W was tattooed into the back. It was the symbol of The Way.

Lankowski and the other man dragged Lawson across the room and seated him upright. They worked quickly to duct tape Lawson's arms and legs against the wooden chair. His head hung forward and he looked at his lap. For the first time since the explosion, he was able to survey some of the damage. He was bleeding badly from his right thigh.

Grizzly stepped into view and yanked Lawson's head up by his hair. The pain in his neck quadrupled as they locked eyes.

"Bet you didn't think when you woke up this morning that it'd be your last." Grizzly smiled. The same smile he'd had just before shooting Hicks.

TEN

THEY LANDED AT TED STEVENS INTERNATIONAL AIRPORT IN Anchorage and rolled to a private strip set aside for restricted access. The sky opened above, and Hatch stared up toward the heavens. Distant flood lights washed out the sky. Beyond their reach, heavy storm clouds threatened.

Two blacked-out Land Rover Defenders were waiting on the tarmac. Less than a minute from when their boots hit the ground, Cruise and team, plus Hatch, were in motion.

Tracy drove the lead vehicle. After a quick three round match of rock, paper, scissors, Hertzog won the coveted passenger seat, giving the big man an extra hour plus of rest time before the show began. Cruise and Hatch sat in the back. Ginger kept his nose tight on Tracy's heels as they raced at breakneck speeds toward Lawson's glacier prison, Camp Hope.

"I've got everybody patched," Tracy announced. "I'm taking you off my earpiece. The others should be able to hear you now. Guys, this is Gerry Cantrell over at intel. He's been filling me in on the situation on the ground, and I want you to hear it directly from him. Gerry, they're all yours."

"Thanks Jordan. How am I coming in? Can everybody here me on your end?" Cantrell spoke quickly like he'd just downed three cups of coffee. Maybe he had. They'd landed in Anchorage later than antici-pated, hitting the ground just after 10 PM. It was close to midnight as they closed in on the last few miles of the drive.

"Good here," Ginger said.

"Loud and clear. Go ahead, Gerry." Tracy kept his eyes on the road as he pushed the pace of the SUV, reaching speeds over ninety as he navigated the slick two-lane mountain roadway like a NASCAR driver pushing the final stretch.

"All right, everybody. I was just telling Commander Tracy about the volatile shitstorm you guys are walking into. And I'm not talking about the bad guys. I'm talking about the environment. I don't know how much you know about Anchorage, but it's a hotbed of seismic activity.

"1964, Anchorage saw an earthquake hit a magnitude of nine-point-two on the Richter scale. It was a megathrust earthquake. That means you've got a massive plate shift and there was massive move-ment. And in four and a half minutes, it became one of the deadliest and most devastating earthquakes in history, second most powerful in the whole world. In that four and a half minutes, over one-hundred-thirty-one lives were lost. The damage, quakes, and seismic activity were felt as far away as Texas."

"We already know about the quake earlier today," Cruise said.

"That wasn't a quake. Well, it was. But not a big one. Four-point-one in magnitude. No major damage. You might've felt like you were having a flashback, made you wobbly for a second, or something."

"Then what are we missing?" Cruise rolled his eyes at Hatch and made a "move it along" gesture with his hand.

"I've been checking the charts and I think we're looking at some-thing else. I think what we witnessed in the quake earlier was a fore-shock. Like a foreshadowing of a much bigger event to come."

"A warning shot," Hatch said under her breath.

"Exactly. And like a warning shot, we need to take heed." Cantrell's voice became even more animated as he continued. Hatch imagined his hands doing most of the talking. "Sometimes before a big quake, you get a ripple of thirty or forty smaller quakes. Some of which are so insignificant people don't even feel them. It can create a ripple effect in which these smaller quakes trigger larger ones. The town of Breakneck is just south of the Aleutian Trench. The Border Ranges Fault Line and Neogene faults that divide the Kenai Peninsula are directly beneath the camp."

"Layman's terms?" Cruise asked.

"Long and short of it, your team is heading into some seriously dangerous ground."

"No way we're letting that marshal die on that glacier." Cruise made no gestures, didn't roll his eyes. There was no swaying the man. "My team's going to bring him down that mountain. Alive."

Cantrell started to speak, paused, and exhaled. "And I wouldn't expect any less. All I'm saying is do it quickly. Anchorage got hit bad in '64. This could be worse. Much worse if the data is to be believed."

"How long do we have?" Cruise looked down at his watch.

"No way to tell. Could be minutes, hours, or years."

"A lot of what we do on the ops side of the house has to do with trusting your gut," Tracy said. "What's yours telling you?"

"You know I can't say with any real accuracy, but my gut is telling me soon. I think we could see some major ground shifts over the next twenty-four hours. If I'm right, then all I can say is make every second on that mountain count."

"We always do. If anything changes on this, I want to know immediately. You've got a direct line to me. Understood?"

"Will do." Cantrell disconnected.

Tracy slowed the Land Rover. The storm had rolled in. Between swipes of the wipers, Hatch saw the wooden sign alongside the road. Breakneck 5 miles. Somebody had spray painted over the words beneath it by crossing out the word 'camp' and replacing it with a 'no'. It read, 'No Hope 7 miles.'

Slick roads were a sign of the loosening grip of winter was giving way to a spring. Long months of cold had left the mountains capped in ice and snow, but the lower foothills were starting to feel the Alaskan warmth of spring. The frozen blanket had begun to melt away, leaving a trail of muddy sludge across the town's main road.

They pulled to a stop by a log cabin with a hand carved wooden sign that hung outside the porch, marking it as Gentry's Pantry.

"Our contact from Parole should be here in a minute." Tracy said to Hatch before turning his attention to Cruise. "Do what you do best."

Cruise exited the vehicle. Hatch met him outside. The heavy rain slapped at her coat as they stood facing each other. She angled her face down to keep the frigid drops away.

"Back before you know it." Cruise leaned in and said in a whisper, "Don't disappear on me."

She inhaled his familiar scent. The scent of the ocean mixing with the rain and wind. Hatch felt like there was something she was supposed to say. She felt like there was more implied in what he was saying. But all she could come up with was, "You'd just end up finding me if I did."

"You're right about that." Cruise leaned closer and kissed Hatch on the lips.

She didn't pull away. Even though it only lasted a second, she could still feel it as the others exited the vehicle. A moment later, Cruise won the next round of rock, paper, scissors, banishing Hertzog to the backseat.

Hatch looked to Tracy to see if he caught the lightening-quick surprise kiss delivered with Navy SEAL-like precision. Nothing about his face indicated he had noticed, but Hatch couldn't have been more grateful to the gray GMC Denali marked with the Board of Parole seal that had pulled to a stop in front of them.

"Looks like our friend from Parole has arrived," Tracy said.

Hatch pulled up her jacket's hood and stood next to Tracy. The rain banged loudly on the waterproof material. Wind found its way through small openings and cooled the back of her neck.

The parole officer approached using a manila file folder as an umbrella. He then extended a wet palm to both Tracy and Hatch.

"Brandon Case, I'm MacIntosh's parole officer. You must be Officer, or is it Agent Hatch?" Case was shorter than Hatch by six inches. He was squat and looked thicker than he was due to the puffy hooded coat he wore.

"Just Hatch is fine by me."

"Your office or mine?" Case laughed at his own joke and took his glasses from the end of his nose. He began wiping the lenses with a cloth only to return them to his face just to watch them fog again.

Tracy would be monitoring Cruise and his team from the Land Cruiser. "Yours is fine."

"Then let's not spend any more time in the rain." Case stepped off in the direction of his truck.

She remembered her task. Find out why a former Marine would end up with a group of Aryan drug dealers capable of killing one officer and kidnapping another. Hatch trailed behind Case, hoping he held the answer.

ELEVEN

Rough hands gripped Lawson's head, and Grizz's thick fingers twisted in the curls of Lawson's hair. His scalp burned as the big man gave one last tug before releasing him. His head fell forward. A sharp stinging sensation shot along the right side of his neck. Lightheaded from blood loss and the trauma he'd endured, Lawson fought to remain conscious. Although, part of him wanted to let go. Two things kept him alive. His wife and his unborn baby girl.

"Wake up, Deputy U.S. Marshal Darren Lawson." Grizz tossed the wallet with his credentials onto the floor in front of him. The worn leather wallet his wife had gotten when he'd first been hired as a deputy. It flopped open, revealing the small replica badge like the one he wore. He remembered how proud she'd been. Now, the polished silver acted as a catch basin, collecting the blood steadily flowing from Lawson's damaged body.

"Your wife looks pretty. Maybe we should stop by and pay her a visit when this is all over." The room laughed. Grizz bent low. His enormous head loomed less than an inch from Lawson's. "Is that what you want me to do?" He pinched Lawson's cheeks between his thumb and forefinger and forced him to look him in the eye. "No? Too bad. What you want doesn't matter anymore."

Lawson gathered the blood pooling in his mouth and spit it into the face of his oversized captor. He never saw Grizz's enormous fist coming. The blow struck against the left side of his head like a runaway Mac truck.

Lawson was now on his side, securely fastened to the chair. That and the paralysis made it impossible to stop the boot that followed. Lawson's vision clouded as a fresh stream of blood trickled across his forehead.

"That's enough!" He recognized the voice of the man who'd carried him up the hill with Lankowski.

"What the hell did you just say to me, boy?" Lawson felt Grizz's words reverberate in the fresh damage to his face.

"This is not The Way that Red described in prison."

Grizz moved across the room in a manner belying the man's size. The other man stood his ground.

"You've been in my presence less time than my last fart and you think you've earned the right to open your dumb mouth?"

"Hold up, Grizz. Let's hear him out."

"Shut up, Frank." Grizz shrugged the man's hand off his shoulder.

"No, you listen to me. MacIntosh did five hard years in Spring Creek's C-Block with Red. That shit means somethin' and you damn well know it."

Grizz took a step back and grunted. His face remained as red as his beard, but his shoulders slumped as the tension eased from his muscles. "Damn you, Winslow."

Frank Winslow then turned his attention to MacIntosh. "Speak your piece. But mind your words, Mac. Few get an audience with the King. Fewer live to talk about it." He aimed a crooked finger that appeared to have been smashed against an opposing lineman's helmet a few times too many. "And I won't stop him a second time."

MacIntosh cleared his throat as his gaze bounced between the others in the room before settling on Grizz. "If you're going to do this guy because he came at you, fine. Get it over with. But I think whatever you have planned is shortsighted."

"Go on." The red on Grizz's cheeks began to fade, returning to their naturally pale state.

"You killed one marshal and kidnapped another. Every law enforcement agency in the country is gunning for you right now. You and Lank are public enemy number one. That means resources are going to be thrown at you like you've never seen."

The room remained silent for a few. All eyes were on MacIntosh.

"Maybe I want them to come." Grizz said.

"Fine if you do. I'll throw down if that's the way this thing breaks." MacIntosh's voice was calm and collected, as if he were arguing a case before a judge. Lawson knew the potential verdict was a death sentence for him. "But at least approach it with a plan of attack instead of flying by the seat of your pants."

"Worked so far, you smart-mouthed bitch." Lankowski squeaked his way into the conversation as he came up along Grizz like a lap dog.

"Shut up!" Grizz delivered an open-handed slap to the back of Lankowski's head with enough force to knock him a few steps forward. He staggered on his wounded foot. Lawson, smiled to himself and wished he'd have put a second round into the man. "I gave Mac the floor. Anybody else feel the need to say their piece?" The room was silent enough for Lawson to hear his droplets of blood hit the badge. "You may continue."

"Leverage. That's what I like in a fight. And no other way about it, there's a fight coming. As much as it sucks, we need to keep this marshal alive if we're to have a chance of holding off the approaching maelstrom."

"We selected this location for a reason," Grizz said. "No cell reception within two miles of here. We're not even a blip on the map."

MacIntosh swung his head side to side. "They'll find you, man. They'll find all of us. No stopping that now. It's not a matter of if, but when."

"Then we cut this piece of shit law dog's throat and lighten our load. Get on our horses and ride."

"It's not going to matter." Grizz shoved Lawson's head with his boot, sending another excruciating wave of pain through the deputy's neck. "Ah, look at him. Somebody brace his damn head so I don't have to bend down to look into the eyes of this piece of shit."

Frank Winslow moved into view, just inside of Lawson's periphery. He had a cruel face, made crueler by a scar nearly dividing one side of his face from the other, leaving the right side a quarter inch higher than the left. Winslow was a living Picasso with hungry eyes. "I say we stick this pig right now!"

"Easy, Frank. I'm not sure his death is exactly what we need right now," Grizz said. "I'm not saying it's off the table, but I like this leverage thing." Grizz pounded his chest like a gorilla. "Today has turned out to be a righteous day. One law dog put down and another in his proper place. More will come and more will fall. I will line the walls of this place with the bodies of our enemies!"

Hicks was dead. A father of seven gunned down. Lawson remained taped to the chair unable to even ball his fist. He resigned himself to grinding his teeth.

"His dead weight is going to slow us down," Lank said. "Look at him. He's already punched full of holes, probably bleed out on us in a minute or two." Lank scurried away before Grizz could land another blow to the scrawny man.

"I don't think so." MacIntosh again asserted himself.

When Grizz turned to face him, it felt as if the earth itself had just shifted on its axis. "And why's that?"

"I've seen people survive worse."

"You some kind of doctor?"

"Medic. Well, I was. Long time ago."

"Continue."

MacIntosh stepped closer like a defense attorney approaching the bench. Lawson held his breath and watched as all eyes in the room shifted to MacIntosh.

Winslow said, "Still don't see why we need to keep this piece of shit alive."

"Because it buys us time," Grizz said. Even when he wasn't pontificating, Grizz's voice rumbled like thunder.

"None of it's going to matter if we don't start plugging those holes and patching him up. He'll be no use to us dead." MacIntosh eyed Lawson.

"How are they even gonna know if he's alive?" Winslow refused to drop his push towards the gallows.

Lawson felt dizzy with dread.

"Proof of life. Take a photo and send it to the cops." MacIntosh was speaking directly to Grizz now, bypassing Winslow.

"I like that. Proof of life." Grizz worked his fingers through a tuft of his thick red beard. "But if we really want to send a message, I think I have something that's a little better than a photograph."

Lawson choked down the fear as Grizz spun. Again, he lowered his face to meet Lawson's. The hot, acrid breath of the behemoth licked at Lawson's nostrils. He fought against the overwhelming desire to close his eyes. Instead, he met the cop killer's cold dead stare with one of his own. "Ready to do your part, Deputy Lawson?" Grizz rose. He directed his next comment at Macintosh. "You any good at fixing people, medic?"

"Good enough."

"I guess we're gonna see about that soon enough." Grizz then turned to another man, standing off to the right. "Buck, take his ear."

"Which one?"

"Does it matter?"

"Guess not."

Lawson put the face to the name as Buck Mathers approached. Lawson's eyes darted to MacIntosh, making a last-minute plea deal. His defense council had rested. The verdict had been rendered.

Mathers drew an eight-inch blade from a leather sheath. The cold steel caught the light from above as it swept by Lawson's face. Mather's hand tugged at Lawson's right ear. The blade disappeared beyond his periphery.

A pain, unlike anything he'd ever experienced, seared a new and horrible memory into this never-ending day as the knife cut into his flesh. A whooshing sound flooded the empty hole where his right ear had been only moments before. Warm blood spilled onto the floor beneath his head.

"Let's give them their proof of life."

Grizz's ominous words were the last Lawson heard before slipping away into darkness.

TWELVE

THE SMELL OF OLD CIGARETTES AND WET DOG PERMEATED THE AIR surrounding Hatch. Evidence of both was littered about the interior cabin of the parole officer's pickup truck. He reached to the backseat and knocked a half-eaten donut off a file, much like the one he'd used as a makeshift umbrella. "Sorry 'bout the mess. I'm gonna tell you what I told your boss when I sent him the digital copy of this file. I'm not sure what you think I can tell you that you don't already know. Hell, I've only met MacIntosh once, during his out processing at Spring Creek."

Hatch wiped the wetness from her hand and extended it toward the file folder. "Mind if I take a look?"

"He's a two-time loser looking at his third and final strike." Case handed over the file. He grimaced and looked at the clock on the car stereo. It was nearly half past midnight. "Do you know how long this is going to take?"

"Hot date?" Hatch said.

"Hey look, I get a call from my supervisor telling me to meet up with agents working on a case with one of my guys and I'm gonna go. But I also don't like wasting my time. What use am I to you now?"

"I won't take any more time than I need. Something about

MacIntosh doesn't sit right." Hatch perused the contents of the file. He had two arrests nearly one year apart. The first for assault. The second for manslaughter. "Tell me about these arrests."

"The first one was actually three different assaults rolled into one case. He messed up three gang bangers. Bad. One of them is blind in one eye."

"Weapons?"

"Nope. Unless you count hands and feet."

"Why was he only sentenced to one year?"

Case's glasses fogged, and he cleaned them on his shirt. "Never got a chance to ask him. MacIntosh skipped out on his first official parole meeting outside the walls a week ago. That's where I usually do the deep dive with these guys to see if they're going to make it on the outside. Civilian life is different once you've been in. Situations, you know. You don't act the way you used to. Everything that happens does so through a different filter. It's...tinted, if that makes sense."

Hatch nodded along. "Sounds a lot like leaving the military."

"Never served myself, but I imagine so. It's a major adjustment. I can say I've seen far more who can't adjust than can. Looks like our friend MacIntosh is proving this to be true."

"Maybe." Hatch continued to stare at the file.

"Maybe? He may have been justified when he busted those three guys. I don't know. He may have truly been defending himself and ended up killing the guy inside. I'm less inclined to believe that one. Again, I wasn't there, so I don't know." He adjusted his glasses and waited for Hatch to look up at him before continuing. "What I do know is survival. Inside, that means one thing, joining a gang."

Hatch had begun to surmise this about MacIntosh. She fished for more information. "What about the manslaughter charge? If I'm reading this right, MacIntosh had one month before he was scheduled for release. Why ruin that?"

"Three weeks." Case shook his head.

"How does a guy get that close and suddenly hit the reset button, adding another five years? Fear of the outside? I mean, does that make sense? He wasn't in the system that long. Right?"

"Killed a guy by snapping his neck." Case tapped out a cigarette from a crumpled American Spirit box that had been resting atop the dashboard. He rolled the cigarette around his stained fingers.

"Who did he kill?"

"An inmate, Baron Dyson. He came at MacIntosh in the yard. He had a shiv. MacIntosh did not, but in the end stood victorious."

Hatch imagined the scenario playing out a few different ways but, in the end, came to the same conclusion about each. "Sounds like an open-and-closed case of self-defense."

Case shrugged and turned his hands palms up. "I guess the judge didn't see it that way. MacIntosh proved him right."

"What's that even mean?" Hatch said. "Proved him right."

"MacIntosh joined up with The Way shortly after killing Dyson. Personally, I think MacIntosh was tasked with killing Dyson by fella named Red Winslow. Red was Grizz's right-hand man until he got locked up. Now his brother Frank's stepped up."

"You know a lot about The Way."

"Working in parole, you hear everything."

Hatch flipped through the folder again. "Doesn't sound like a two-time loser to me."

Case laughed and looked up at her from under his glasses. "You gotta be kidding me, right? He crippled three men and killed another. Regardless of the circumstances, this guy shouldn't be out and about. And now look, we've got a dead marshal and the gang he's tied in with is responsible. Trust me lady, MacIntosh is going back in and he's never going to see the light of day again."

"You mentioned you didn't serve. But this is a DD214?" Hatch held up a single sheet of paper.

"I saw."

"Nothing stood out as odd to you?"

"Lots of criminals have served in the military."

"True. There're bad apples in every profession."

Case rubbed his brow in frustration and stuck the unlit cigarette in his mouth. "What makes him so different?"

"For starters, he was honorably discharged. Secondly, he was a combat medic with two tours overseas with a Force Recon unit. It just doesn't jibe. Why would somebody who's spent his life saving people be involved with a violent group of murderers? Something doesn't add up."

Case offered a slight smile. "You're looking for something that isn't there. I've seen it a thousand times before. The bars change people and not for the better. Recidivism is on the rise. And here in Alaska it's no different."

Hatch continued to look at the copy of MacIntosh's military discharge paperwork. One word stood out from all the rest. Honorable.

"If there's nothing else…" Case shot an eye toward the clock and fumbled with his lighter. "Nasty habit, but it's about time for my nic fix."

"Thanks for your time."

"I can tell you're not convinced. Whatever his reason, mere association automatically violates his parole. When Chris MacIntosh comes down that mountain, it's gonna be in cuffs. Good luck."

"Luck favors the prepared." Hatch exited the vehicle into the swirling wind and sleet. The frigid air worked its way into any opening it could find. She made her way back to Tracy's Land Rover. The Talon commander turned when she entered and looked at her with raised eyebrows.

"Anything good?"

"Case has written off Macintosh as a byproduct of the prison system."

"And you don't?"

"No."

"Well, Cruise can ask him that in about fifteen minutes. The team's on the ATV trail now. Should be on foot shortly."

Case drove off as a rust covered Ford E350 van pulled into the spot where Case's pickup had been only moments before. Radars and satellite dishes and antennae of varying lengths poked out from the roof top like a porcupine having a bad hair day.

The wiper blades cleared the windshield and Hatch stared out at the man who had exited a storm tracker vehicle wearing an old Navy flight suit and a red and black plaid wool-lined hat with the flaps pulled down. He got down on all fours and put his head near the muddy road.

"You get a lot of crazies living up in these parts. Recluses, lost touch with their sanity."

Hatch thought of Jed Russell who lived near Hawk's Landing, and how wrong she'd been about him when she'd first rushed to that conclusion.

The windshield filled with the slushy sleet, obscuring the crouched man. Hatch returned her attention to the monitor in front of them. The drone image showed thermal signatures as the skies darkened. Cruise and his team moved toward their objective.

"We've left the main road. The ATV trail is a mud run." Cruise came through the car's speaker system. There was heavy static and the comms dropped.

Tracy made some adjustments to the digital tablet he was tracking them on. "We've still got you on visual. State police have the drone up. All heat signatures are still showing at the target location."

"Pour me a beer and we'll be back before the head settles. Cruise and team out for now."

The screen flickered. Thunder louder than any Hatch had ever heard rumbled. A second later, the strange man and his van disappeared.

The windshield disintegrated. Bits of glass showered Hatch and Tracy as the Land Rover was swallowed by the churning ground.

Tracy grunted in pain. She saw his left leg had been trapped awkwardly under the brake pedal. His shin was twisted in the opposite direction of his thigh.

The front end was pulled deeper. The shattered screen of the tablet flickered like a strobe light and then went out. The silence that followed was short lived.

Nose down fifteen feet below where the road had once been, Hatch heard a new sound. The loud rushing sound of water filled the air.

THIRTEEN

THE FAUCET HAD BEEN MAKING THAT SOUND FOR MONTHS, AND LAWSON had promised to fix it for just as long. It was what they'd been arguing about before he had left for the office. He knew it wasn't really about the faucet. All it needed was a washer. He was handy enough. He just hadn't had the time.

Now time was running out on him. Things began to slow. He fought through the heavy fog coating his brain and dulling his senses. He focused on holding the image of his wife's face in his mind. But it was her last words to him that fueled his will to live.

I hate you.

She's said it immediately after hurling a jar of bread and butter pickles at him. Her aim had been off, intentionally, or unintentionally, he didn't know. It broke against the wall of their two-bedroom apartment.

Lawson knew Bonnie didn't hate him. She hated him for dragging her away from everything she loved so he could play cops and robbers, chasing a dream that had proven to be a nightmare he still hadn't awakened from.

Bonnie's words played on an endless loop. *I hate you.* Lawson would be damned if those were the last words he heard from his wife. He waged the fight of his life, willing himself forward. Lawson looked down at the puddle of blood and wished he could be back in his undecorated kitchen standing back in the broken glass and pickle juice.

"See if there's more supplies in the kitchen." MacIntosh cleared blood from Lawson's face.

"I ain't your bitch, you hear me?" Lankowski was pacing behind MacIntosh. His feet slapped the floor. "Just 'cause Grizz left me in here doesn't mean I work for you."

MacIntosh continued working on the injured man. "I'm trying to plug these holes to stop the bleeding. I need you to go get me the med supplies."

Lankowski pulled a nickel-plated .38 caliber snub nose Smith and Wesson revolver from behind his back. He tapped it against the steel of his oversized rodeo belt buckle. "This gun here says I ain't got to do shit but sit here and watch."

MacIntosh turned his head and eyed the pistol in Lankowski's hand. "Might want to put that down before you shoot yourself in the other foot."

"I told you that piece of shit pig shot me!" Lankowski pointed the gun at Lawson who was duct taped to the back of the chair and could do nothing but stare down the barrel. Or close his eyes. Lawson chose to look death in the eye. Lankowski stared with his bloodshot eyes. He had a deranged look about him. His pacing became more erratic. His thin arm jabbed outward, delivering thrusts from the pistol pointed cockeyed out in front of him.

Lawson heard MacIntosh release a long, slow exhale. A calm settled over his face. "Hang tight," he said in a voice for only Lawson to hear. MacIntosh stood and turned. His body shielded Lawson, but Lankowski continued to pop in and out of view as he paced, the gun flailing about.

"You point that thing in my direction one more time and you'll be the one in that chair when Grizz gets back."

"What'd you say?" Lankowski flailed his arms, but Lawson could see the weapon was no longer pointed their way. "I've got a right mind to whoop your pig luvin' ass, right here, right now."

"Nothing between us but air and opportunity." MacIntosh shifted his weight, balling his fist as he did so. Lankowski didn't notice. But Lawson did. "Choose wisely. Once you cross that line there's no coming back."

The whooshing of his pulse was the only thing Lawson heard for the next several seconds while dead air lay between the two men in a standoff before him. Lankowski laughed, sounding more bird than human.

"What is it with you and this cop? Shit, you didn't offer me any help when I came in with a shot foot. Look at this damn thing. I got it wrapped in a dirty ass dishrag. Why didn't you lift a finger to help with the bullet in my foot?"

"Because I don't like you."

"And you like him?"

"No. You should have listened earlier when school was in session. This cop is a means to an end. That end being not getting arrested or killed. He's leverage and you're dead weight." A ripple of muscle shot up MacIntosh's right arm. His balled fist tightened. "Plus, I have a thing for assholes. But you know what really pisses me off? Skinny tweakers who have big balls when they're around bigger men or have a gun in their hand. Take those things away and you're nothing but a cockroach."

Lankowski stood silent.

"Shit or get off the pot. Throw down or put that piece away. The longer you wait, the more explaining you're gonna have to do to Grizz when he gets back and finds the leverage is gone. He's out there right now, delivering this cop's ear as a message. What do you think a man like Grizz will do to a pissant piece of shit like you when he finds out? Hell, he doesn't even trust you with anything more powerful than that five round pea shooter."

"At least he lets me carry one. He doesn't trust you enough to give you one." Frothy spit flew from Lankowski's mouth as he yelled.

"Maybe not. Or maybe he knows firsthand what I did in Spring

Creek to Dyson. He had a knife. I didn't. He's dead. I'm not. Maybe, Grizz hasn't given me a gun because he knows I'm deadly enough without one."

Lankowski squawked again. He then tucked the gun behind his back. "Man, you're an asshole. But you're right, this piece of shit law dog ain't gonna die on my watch. You and I will settle up later."

"Looking forward to it. Until then, how about you help me by finding supplies while I keep pressure on the wounds?"

"That ain't gonna happen. First off, I don't know what the hell I should be lookin' for. If I did, my foot wouldn't be lookin' like a blind doctor with one hand did my bandages." Lankowski stepped forward. The light cast a shadow on his bony face, making his nearly translucent skin more ghoulish. "I don't mind putting pressure on this fine upstanding lawman's wounds. In fact, it'd be my pleasure."

"You put pressure here, here, and here. Like this." MacIntosh turned and demonstrated. Lawson could only feel the juggle of his head and nothing else. "The harder the pressure, the better. He's not going to feel it either way. That bullet in his trap did something bad."

Lankowski exchanged an exaggerated salute. "Sir, yes sir."

"No funny stuff." Macintosh disappeared from Lawson's periphery.

Lankowski waited until it was quiet. The swooshing in Lawson's head continued to pulse, but it was now quiet and much slower. "Nothing funny 'bout getting shot in my foot is there? How 'bout we make it even? What's that old sayin'…an eye for an eye? That's it! How 'bout I take your eye?"

Help! Lawson tried to yell. He was too weak to push his voice past his lips.

Lankowski stepped back and undid the black leather belt from his jeans. His pants sagged to the midway point on his boxer briefs while he wrapped the belt around his right fist. The belt buckle lay atop a coiled snake of leather. A silver cowboy waving his hat on top of a bucking bronco was the last image Lawson saw in the moment before it collided with the left side of his face.

Lawson's world upended. The blow knocked him backward. He looked up at the ceiling tiles; the white squares held in place by thin strips of wood made it look like a tic-tac-toe board. Lankowski floated into view. The belt buckle, the silver cowboy now crimson, hurtled down.

Lawson took in a breath and was prepared for it to be his last. In his exhale he imagined his final words being invisibly sent to his wife. Lawson said what he should have before he left for work. I'm sorry.

Lankowski's belt buckle blotted out the light as it closed in for the finishing blow. Both of Lawson's eyes were now nearly swollen shut and the slits he could see through were filled with blood. He blinked clear his left eye to see the red cowboy buckle disappearing to his right, along with the man holding it.

Lawson strained to see out of the corner of his right eye. MacIntosh was on top. Lawson silently cheered on his defense-attorney-turned-champion as he rained down a hailstorm of punches on Lankowski's face. Lankowski held up his left arm to deflect some of the blows. The gun was in his other hand and pointed in MacIntosh's face.

Lankowski pulled the trigger. MacIntosh shifted his head. Bits of the ceiling tile above rained down from the bullet's hole.

Before the white flecks hit the ground, MacIntosh had stripped the revolver from Lankowski's hand. He moved incredibly fast, flowing from one move to another. He trapped Lankowski's extended hand, the one which he'd taken the gun from. With a quick twist of his body, MacIntosh snapped his elbow. Lankowski let out a shriek. Before he could articulate his anger into words beyond the train of expletives rolling out of his mouth, Lankowski was silenced by a devastating forearm blow to the side of his neck.

MacIntosh wasted no time. He tucked the revolver into the small of his back and stood. He reached down and grabbed Lankowski by the pant legs and dragged him out the front door.

Lawson used the dripping of his blood to mark the passage of time. MacIntosh walked back through the same door he'd dragged Lankowski out of. He hustled over to Lawson and took a knee.

"Lankowski?" Each letter scraped across the back of Lawson's throat as he forced out the question.

"I told him next time he pointed that thing at me he'd be the one in a chair. I always keep my promises. I just found a seat more suitable for someone of his stature." MacIntosh's lips curled ever so slightly. "Now, let's see about getting you patched up."

The ground shook and a loud cracking sound, like that of a hundred trees snapping in half at the same time, filled the quiet.

FOURTEEN

THE HANGAR HAD BEEN CONVERTED TO A MOCKUP OF THE campground's cafeteria. The dimensions were marked off with tape across the linoleum floor, and office partitions had been used for walls with gaps left for the entry points. They'd been running the drill non-stop since arriving in Anchorage. The only breaks occurred during the debriefs, the last of which had lasted five minutes. The teams were staged for another run when a loud boom rumbled across the tarmac like thunder.

"What the hell was that?" Kevin Medina caught himself on Babz.

"Nothing good." Babz stabilized both herself and Medina. She looked around for the source of the disruption. "Were we bombed?"

"Get used to it." Hoop shouted over the noise of a taxiing plane. "If we get the green light, this is the environment we'll be operating in, so this is the environment we train in. Now let's run it again. Team one, stack up. On my command...Execute!"

Babz stayed tight. She was the proverbial fifth wheel, literally the fifth person on a four-man team designed to make a dynamic entry. They stayed tight, but not so much that they could trip. But as soon as one stopped or halted, they had to be on each other's hip.

"Execute means staying tight."

Gaps meant time, and time in life and death situations was everything. The more sands in the hourglass, the better your odds of survival.

Never move faster than you can shoot.

Babz posted up behind Medina. Once the point man had stopped, Babz tapped up her non-gun hand to smack the back left hip of Medina, who in turn sent it up the chain until the "Good to go" message was received by the point man.

Her Glock 35 long barrel with laser sight and trigger modifications was in the Sul position pressed low at the center of her chest. A few seconds later, Hoop banged a drum loudly to simulate the sound of a flashbang. Babz thrummed with energy as she surged forward with her team. Their movement was fast and precise as they launched into the open door. The ammunition in their weapons had been exchanged for real action die markers, which were accurate in close quarters. They showed shots placed and gave simulated impact, marking the target where you hit it.

And these were live targets who would shoot back with the same markers.

Babz moved in. She could hear the suppressed sound of the simulation fired by members of her team. Her focus was on her lane, and as Medina shifted left, he missed sight of a target who'd popped out from behind a large cabinet in the kitchen area.

Babz fired three shots in a matter of a split second, two striking center of mass, the third hitting the visor. A red dot of splattered die marker paint was dead center between his eyes.

"Time!" Hoop called. "Twenty-two seconds from movement to door to entry to elimination of all targets and safe rescue of the hostage."

Medina looked at the shooter who would've shot him, and then back at Babz. He opened his mouth to speak when Hoop interrupted and moved himself between them and the target that Babz had eliminated.

"Let me guess, you were about to say something to her like, 'It should be you going in on this assault team and not me'?"

Medina, a man of confidence, looked shell-shocked. "I was just gonna say it was a hell of a shot and..."

"And?" Hoop's eyes narrowed. "You're stammering, Medina. Save yourself the embarrassment and shut your mouth." Hoop's attention swiveled to Babz like he was sizing her up in his scope. "Do you think you deserve a shot on the assault team, should this thing get the green light?"

Babz felt a tremor, but she contained it. She knew what he was doing. He was looking for an answer, and she had to make sure she gave the right one. "Medina goes."

"You're just saying that because I put you on the spot."

"No, Medina goes because when it mattered, he won." Babz's father had taught her that philosophy early on. Redos don't happen in real life. "If you don't win when it matters, it doesn't matter when you win."

Hoop paused for a moment. "Sounds like your father taught you well." He leaned back and addressed everyone. "That's right, boys and girls. Your shots don't count in this room if they don't work when the pressure's on. You better rise to it or you won't be here long." Hoop turned and almost ran into Brett Larson. "Larson? What do you need?"

"Your team needs to saddle up."

"Say again?"

"Hoop, you're the show now. I just got word."

Hoop's chest puffed out as he turned to address the room, but Larson stopped him. "You're not going in on the assault just yet. The other team is down. Landslide."

Hoop appeared rattled by the information. "Are they still alive?"

"Unknown. Your team is going to be the rescue. Only way in at this point is by helicopter. You're going to have to use one of those choppers as medevac. Anchorage has the closest major hospital with a helipad, but you'll have to be the one to get them there."

"What about Lawson?"

"It's going to have to wait. There's going to be no assault mission until these quakes settle. I need you to put together a rescue team and get to that LZ. The assault team will remain on standby, but from the looks of it..." Larson cast a glance around at all the die markers on the bad guys, and not one on any of the entry team members. "If it comes to that, you've got assault in the bag."

"I'll pull a few guys and run the rescue." Hoop clasped a firm hand on Bill Sykes' shoulder. "Have the assault team get some rest. Because when I get back, I'm going to push like hell to get us in there so we can get that marshal the hell out."

Sykes agreed with a nod.

"Wren, Medina, and Babz, you heard Larson. This is a rescue mission. Now get your ass in a chopper, you're coming with me."

Medina took one last look at the target he should've seen.

Babz gave him a gentle nudge. "You won't miss it when it counts."

Shaking his head, he said, "I hope you're right."

"I am." She leaned in close to Medina and whispered. "When you go out there, you make it count."

FIFTEEN

Breakneck was surrounded by four lakes, Ptarmigan, Grant, Crescent, and Kenai. The biggest of the four was the Kenai. It ran parallel to the main road through town and up the mountain to Camp Hope. That road, or at least the portion where Hatch and Tracy had been sitting, dropped fifteen feet. Mud was the only view from the crushed front windshield. The vehicle was nose down. The ground swallowed the front end.

Hatch was slammed about the cabin when the ground shift occurred and came to a final resting place mashed into the dashboard with her left forearm wedged between the dash and shattered windshield. She worked her arm free, ignoring the pain of sliced skin. After clearing bits of broken glass that had penetrated her jacket and her flesh, she assessed herself. Minus some minor lacerations, she had no broken bones and was, by all accounts unharmed.

A low grunt came from Tracy, his voice imperceptible over the water rushing in. Hatch could feel the frigid water battling against her water-resistant boots as she twisted to face Tracy.

"How bad?" Hatch asked.

Tracy was bent forward, holding his left leg at the knee. "Dislocated. No break. Tracy roared as he yanked his ankle free from the pedal. His lower leg dangled loosely.

The sound of rushing water was replaced by another. Wind howled through the broken SUV. Hatch's eyes widened when she saw the source. As she adjusted to the disorienting darkness, Hatch realized the wind whipping against the outside of the SUV preceded a massive wall of water. The normally placid Kenai sent a tidal wave their way. And it was closing in fast.

Hatch looked at the injured Tracy and then at their escape route through the Land Rover's rear window. She was out of what she needed most. Time.

"Brace for impact!" Hatch climbed into the backseat. She wedged herself between the seats but kept her body loose. Tense muscles and locked joints meant tears and broken bones.

The sound was deafening, like a hundred firehoses hitting at once. The Land Rover held its ground. Or better yet, the ground held the Land Rover. The raging water met the wall of earth like a boxer's punch, landing an overhand right to a heavy bag. And Hatch and Tracy were smack dab in the middle.

The reinforced frame maintained the vehicle's structural integrity. The bullet resistant windows survived. However, the shattered front windshield was all but washed away. Muddy water flooded the interior compartment.

"Where's your gun?" she yelled.

"Center console." He mashed a black button set inside a panel of lacquered wood. Nothing happened. His face reddened. "Low profile admin bullshit."

Hatch positioned herself with her back to the rear window. She lowered the middle row and squeezed in. Hatch braced the inside of her forearms against the seatbacks. "Be ready to move when I breach that window!"

Hatch delivered a mule kick. The shock wave resonated from her heel along her spine. The window remained intact.

"Those windows are designed to take a hell of a beating, but they are also designed for rapid egress. With the weight of that water, you're gonna have to kick like hell." Tracy yelled as the water worked its way past his waist. He grunted as he climbed into the backseat compartment. Tracy rested against the back of the passenger seat. Debris from the river floated across the surface.

Cold water surged into the cabin, sounding like a mini-Niagara Falls. The front of the vehicle was completely submerged. Hatch figured they had less than a minute until they would be drowned. As Hatch braced for another kick, something stung her left arm. She reached down and found another piece of glass. Hatch pulled out a shard no bigger than her thumbnail. She was about to toss it when she had an idea.

The dark, muddy water surrounding the Land Rover on all sides continued to rise. Hatch stuffed the piece of glass into her right boot heel. She shot her foot backward. A deafening crack sounded. Shattered glass gave way to a waterfall of brown river water.

She was cast in an icy darkness. Hatch held her breath and felt her way over to where Tracy had been. She swung her arm in search of him, instead finding the leather of the passenger seat where he'd been only a moment ago. Desperate, she continued to search the empty seat.

Hatch twisted herself through the seats where she'd been wedged. She swam down deeper where she found him unmoving. Hatch moved quickly, navigating her way by touch. She worked an arm under his shoulder. Using the seatback for leverage, Hatch hoisted the Talon commander into the backseat. Her lungs burned. She fought through the pain, clawing her way to the back.

Just as Hatch got herself through the rear window, the ground shifted with the sound of grating metal and tossed the Land Rover to the left. Tracy slipped free. Hatch lost contact. Her lungs hit the point of no return. She launched herself upward, springing off the door.

As Hatch broke through to the surface, she inhaled as much water as air on her first breath. Her lungs screamed in rebellion. On the second inhalation, she was replenished enough to make the dive.

The back end of the SUV was six feet below the newly formed waterline. Hatch pulled her upper body through the window she'd just extricated herself from. Tracy lay against the backseat. Hatch pulled Tracy up. She dipped to his midline and, with a burst of effort, shoved him up and out of the rear compartment. Her lungs burned worse than before. She hadn't grabbed enough oxygen. The hypoxic effects started to cloud her mind.

Hatch pulled Tracy tight to her body and stood up on the back end. She then squatted low and brought him over her right shoulder. Hatch exploded with all the force her body could muster.

She broke through to the surface with Tracy. Her left hand clawed at the dirt as she climbed to the road. Bits of asphalt broke off, and she slid down along the mud wall and back into the water.

Hatch kicked her feet until she felt the Land Rover under her again. She pushed off once more as the SUV sank deeper into the widening crevasse. The last-minute shifting of the vehicle threw off her momentum, and she slammed into the mud beneath the road.

She tore fresh hand holds into the mud and climbed with Tracy slung over her shoulder. Her head broke through the churning water. She inhaled deeply. Rejuvenated by the oxygen, she threw her arm onto the wet asphalt. She adjusted Tracy's body to keep his head above water. He had a gash on the side of his head, which bled heavily. His dead weight was stopping them from reaching the summit.

Tracy then coughed wildly. His convulsions yanked Hatch downward. She lost her contact with the road's surface and was riding a mudslide into unforgiving floodwater. Tracy pulled her down into the black water. Her head submerged again. Hatch raked her hand across the earth wall, desperate to find purchase amid the churning water. There was none.

She refused to release the man. Hatch continued to fight. As the Kenai River pulled them under water, something yanked Hatch upward.

SIXTEEN

STRONG HANDS PULLED HER AND TRACY ONTO THE ROAD.

Hatch fought to catch her breath as she watched the strange man in the plaid hat and aviator's jacket deliver five quick rescue breaths to Tracy. The Talon commander lay flat on his back. His leg bent awkwardly. The dislocated knee had not been reset, and if it wasn't soon, his leg could be lost. That wasn't the priority. Getting Tracy to breathe again was.

Red and black plaid flaps slapped Tracy's chin as the man moved in to deliver another round of breaths. Tracy coughed a lungful of water into his rescuer's face. He sat up with assistance.

Hatch moved to the other side. She performed a quick assessment, starting with Tracy's head. "Take it slow. You've got a pretty nasty gash on the side of your head there." Hatch moved her way down to his injured knee. She ran her hand from his ankle up to shin. "No breaks that I can feel. Looks like it's just the knee."

"Got to put it back in place." Tracy grimaced as he poked around the kneecap bulging on the outside of the joint. "Care to do the honors?"

Hatch gripped his ankle and straightened it as far as the dislocated knee would allow. She elevated the knee off the ground. "Ready?"

Tracy nodded. Hatch then bent the knee inward. Tracy grunted through grit teeth. A pop sounded and she felt the kneecap slip back into place.

"Not the Baywatch moment I'd envisioned as a kid, but I'd take it over the alternative any day of the week." Tracy cackled at his own joke as he let go of his injured knee and extended a hand toward the stranger. "Appreciate the assist."

"Don't mention it." Hair the color of smoke hung connected to a long, thick beard. Water ran off the plaid flaps. He looked like a wet sheep dog. "Didn't do much but lend a hand. I'm sure you'd do the same. She's the one you should be thanking."

Tracy shifted his attention to Hatch. "My tablet was in the Land Rover. I'll reach out to headquarters and get a status update. And give them ours." Tracy pulled the phone from his wet pocket. White light turned the sleet into falling diamonds. The screen cast shadows on the scowl etched across his face. "Shit."

"What is it?" Hatch looked at the screen for answers but couldn't make anything out through the beads of water.

"Text from Cruise."

Hatch moved closer. Tracy shared the screen.

Compromised. Landslide. Taylor's dead. Not sure on Hertzog. Pinned by a boulder. Op is a no-go.

Tracy shot a quick reply. *Hang tight. We're coming for you.* He made a call. "Looks like you and your boys are up to bat. Landslide hit my team. Yeah. Yeah. They're trapped on the ATV trail. I've got one dead, one MIA, and one who's trapped. I'm going to need to get them off that mountain and to a hospital as fast as possible. I'll send their location. And Hoop, best of luck."

Hatch couldn't believe what she was hearing. "You're turning it over to the FBI? There's no Talon contingency team ready to fill the void?"

Tracy wiped water from his face. "Situations like this don't typically require the manpower. We try to leave a minimal footprint when we put boots on the ground on ops like this one." He searched the sky for answers. "Do you have a better plan?"

"Yes." Hatch looked past Tracy at the van with the antennae poking out in all directions.

"You've got to be kidding me?"

"How long will it take those choppers to get here?"

"Around forty-five minutes from takeoff to landing."

"Does that message from Cruise sound like he's got forty-five minutes?" Hatch stood and helped Tracy to his feet.

"No." He slapped the thigh of his injured leg. "This leg isn't going to make the climb."

"Won't need to. I'm faster on my own." Hatch heard the way it sounded. "Not saying you couldn't hang. It's just how I've been making a go of it since joining civilian life."

Hatch turned to the strange weatherman. "Sir, I hate to do this, especially after what you just did for us. But one way or another, I'm taking that vehicle up that mountain."

"First off, don't call me sir. I work for a living." A seriousness in the man's eyes prefaced his words. "Secondly, nobody drives Jessie but me."

She didn't have time to argue. "It's an emergency."

"Ma'am, no offense, but look around. This seismic activity is being felt for hundreds of miles in every direction. That means thousands of emergencies are happening around the region right now."

"First off, don't call me ma'am, I work for a living, too." Hatch eyed the faded leather of the weatherman's bomber jacket getting a freshwater rinse from the endless rain. The sleeves were lined with military patches spanning all four branches of service. "Do those patches mean something to you?"

"Every single one of them." The man beamed with pride.

"Then I assume it would matter if I told you the people I'm going to save wore a similar patch to the one on your arm, right there?" Amid the smattering of patches, one stood out to Hatch as she attempted to commandeer his van. A stitched image depicted a tattooed frog wearing a sailor's cap and smoking a cigar while carrying two sticks of dynamite. Above it read, *Underwater Demolition Team 12.* UDTs were the primordial ooze used to form the Navy's SEAL teams. Hatch tapped her finger to it.

"Yes ma'am, it would. I still can't let you take Jessie. She's every-thing I have." Before Hatch could make a rebuttal, he snapped to attention and presented a salute, tapping the edge of an index finger to the red and black plaid of his fur-lined trapper cap. "Aerographer's Mate, Third Class, Burton Hill, at your service. If you need to get up that mountain, there's nobody better to get you there than my girl, Jessie. And there's nobody who drives her but me. She's a bit particular."

"I don't care who drives as long as you get me there." Hatch turned to Tracy. "Up for it?"

"I'd just slow you down. Besides, I'm going to need to maintain comms with HRT inbound."

"You can get yourself out of the rain in old man Gentry's place." Hill pointed beyond his van to the log cabin. "Second oldest surviving roadside lodge in the entire Kenai Peninsula. Nearly sixty years it's sat here."

"Looks closed," Tracy said. "But I'm sure I can find my way in."

"No need. The key is under the wood carved bear on the porch. Old Man Gentry did it years back. It's run by his son who lives in Anchorage. He maintains the upkeep on supplies but rarely keeps shop during the winter months. He leaves the key for locals to use while he's away."

"That's some trust." Tracy's southern twang returned. He began limping his way toward the long rectangular cabin.

"No. That's Alaska." Hill opened the door to the van and hopped inside.

Hatch climbed into the passenger seat and closed the door to the rain and wind. The distant sound of the storm sent tingles through her frigid skin. She watched as Tracy ambled up the wooden steps to the porch where the carved bear stood guard beside the front door. He looked over his shoulder and waved. Hatch returned the gesture, then focused on the road ahead.

"And we're off." The tires spun before gaining traction. The Ford E350, better known as Jessie, pulled forward.

"Do you know the ATV trail that runs off the main road outside the entrance to Camp Hope?"

"I know it. That's going to be a tough run for my girl here." Hill drummed his fingers on the steering wheel. "But she's never backed down from a challenge. And I'm not about to change that today."

"You really don't have to do this."

"You asked me if the patches meant something. The one you pointed out belonged to my father. He was on the last UDT demolition mission, Fourth of July 1945 in Balikpapan, Borneo." He shot a glance at the cigar-smoking frog. "So, you see, I really do have to do this."

SEVENTEEN

HILL LOOKED AT HATCH MORE THAN THE ROAD. EVERY TIME THE MAN spoke, which was often, he turned his head to her. She wondered about whether he'd deliver on his promise of getting her up that trail, let alone up the paved road they were currently traveling.

"There might be a towel back there if you need to dry off." Hill pointed to the back.

"No need." Hatch brushed off the slush with her hand as she scanned her surroundings.

Computer monitors and hard drives lined both walls of the rear interior. Some of the monitors were stacked two high. Newspaper clippings and photographs were stuck to the van's walls. Most of the images depicted earthquakes. Several long planks of wood bounced noisily about on the floor liner. Gallons of paint were contained by a cargo net that worked to retain them as the Ford swerved.

"It's my passion." He shook water from his plaid flaps as he turned his head, eyes off the road again, and gave a sheepish shrug. "I'm a quake hunter."

"And how do the paint cans fit in?"

"I need to eat. Following earthquakes doesn't really foot the bill, ya know. I paint houses and do general handy work."

She glanced at the side mirror. "That explains the extendable ladder on the side of the van."

"No room on the roof." Hill raised a hand and patted the roof above his head. The van swerved.

The sleet intensified. Duct tape held the wiper blade together on Hatch's side. It only managed to clear the bottom half of the window, leaving her view blurred.

"How well do you know this area?" she asked.

"Like the back of my hand. Been chasing these little hiccups up and down the fault for years. Breakneck is where I spend much of my time."

"I need you to take me to the ATV trail, preferably close to the glacier. That's where they are."

"Hell, I could take my hands off the wheel and Jessie could get us there by herself." He demonstrated. Wind shoved the van and he quickly brought it under control. "Hang tight. Be at the split in less than five minutes."

"Ever take Jessie off-road?"

Hill laughed. "She can take on anything. Toughest girl I've ever met."

"Got to ask. Jessie?"

"It's a long story for a short ride." This time he kept his gaze focused on the road in front of him. "Probably not old enough to remember, but there was a big quake in Anchorage."

"I was briefed on it."

"Well, whatever they told you couldn't do justice to the true devastation a quake of that magnitude causes."

"You were there?"

Hill nodded. "I can still see it clear as day. Good Friday, 1964. I was only six at the time, but my father had taken me to Cameron's Café on Fourth Ave. Friday nights at Cameron's were the best because I got to spend time with my mom while she worked. With my mom working as a waitress, I was treated like royalty, extra scoops of ice cream, the works. My mom had just slipped into the kitchen to make my sundae."

Hill was quiet for a moment. Whatever visual recall the retelling had evoked, it gave him pause. At least for a moment.

"It was the craziest thing. I remember seeing my mom in the kitchen. In the version I created, she turns to me and blows a kiss my way. In reality, she never looked back. I knew the truth of it then, just as I do now. It was my way of coping with what happened next."

Hatch pictured the scene.

"The crunching sound was deafening, like somebody had thrown a handful of nails into a garbage disposal while it was running. At that age, I was a big Godzilla fan. I swear I thought for a moment he had come to Anchorage.

"I remember sitting there, holding my spoon in gleeful anticipation of my special treat when everything went all topsy-turvy. Not all of it is clear anymore. I'm sure much of it is tucked down deep inside and to be honest, I don't think I'd really want to remember all the details. I know this, my mother died in that kitchen along with the cook. My father tried like hell to claw his way to her, but it was too late. She'd been killed instantly. All because I wanted a sundae."

"You were six." Hatch saw the strain in the man's face and knew, all too well, its burden. "Can't blame yourself."

"I know. There's been a million years between then and now, but it took me a long time to forgive myself for that sundae. I think in some ways my father blamed me, too. You can't be mad at the ground. It's as silly as being mad at the wind and rain. Those are forces outside our control. All we can do is work to understand them. But what we can blame, what we can control, is ourselves. I guess everybody has that moment in life where they find their purpose. Comes I guess at different times for different people. I imagine every circumstance is different, but for me, it was that day, Good Friday 1964, at 5:36 PM. It's strange to be able to go back to that millisecond and time where your whole life fractured."

Hatch nodded. She, too, knew the exact day and time her life changed forever. Her new trajectory had her landing in uncharted territory, but adopting her father's code as a way of life had satiated Hatch's need for purpose. "Did I miss the part where you explained why you call your van Jessie?"

"It's the clearest, unfabricated recall from that day." Hill cleared his throat. "In my father's haste to rush to my mother's aid, he failed to notice my leg was trapped at the ankle by a huge piece of concrete wall that had fallen. I remember calling to him. And then Jessie appeared. Her name tag, centered above her breast pocket of her sky-blue uniform of Cameron's Café, read Jessie. She must've been new, because I'd never seen her before. Never saw her after. We buried my mother the following week and moved to Vermont. But Wendy brought me back."

"Wendy?"

"It's what I named the big one."

"The one in '64?"

Hill shook his head. Jessie shook with him. "Nah. For me, that will always be the *big one*, but that's for reasons you now know. The next big one is coming. I've been trying to get anyone and everyone to listen. Sent my findings to every news station about a million times. They just write me off as some crazy old coot. You know, maybe I am. Who's to say?"

"I think it takes a special kind of crazy to run toward a collapsed roadway to rescue two people you don't know, who were seconds from drowning." She smiled and followed it with a slight bow of her head. "And I will take that kind of crazy any day of the week and twice on Sunday."

Hill ran his hand through the smoky gray of his beard, wringing out some of the accumulated rainwater. "I was scared to come back. And you can read all you want about earthquakes, watch newscasts from around the world, but until you experience firsthand what it's like when the earth just rips out from under you and slams you down fifteen feet, you just don't understand. Those four plus minutes might as well have been four lifetimes."

"But you're here now. You faced your fear."

"I'm facing it right now. Every time I go on the hunt, I feel it with me every step of the way."

"What was it that brought you back?"

"Like I said, my father moved us to Vermont. He wanted to put some serious distance between us and Alaska. I ended up joining the military with the hopes of following in my father's footsteps by joining the Navy. Even tried to get myself into the SEAL program. But the rubble that fell on my ankle in '64 came back to bite me in the ass. It did some serious damage, and I ended up needing surgery. I've got a couple pins in there. Wasn't enough to disqualify me from service, just Spec Warfare. So, I used the military to pursue my other passion. Weather. Earthquakes.

"Named the big one Wendy after the girl who wrote me a Dear John letter while I was overseas, spending my days aboard the aircraft carrier USS Enterprise. '76 to '80, those were some of the best years of my life. During my West Pac deployment, saw a little excitement when we were followed by a Russian Kynda-class rocket cruiser. Followed us around for a few days, kinda scary, but nothing like the action of today. But whatever we lacked for in an action, we sure as hell made up for in general quarters drills.

"But we did some real good, too. We received a distress call that fifteen Taiwanese fishermen were stranded in open water. Probably would've died if our battle group hadn't been there to receive the distress call."

The whole time he spoke, Burton never took his foot off the gas pedal, and he drove wildly, barely looking at the road and making Hatch grateful that the view out the front of her side of the windshield was obscured by the duct taped wiper and its failure to clear her view.

"Don't get me wrong. A 9.2 megathrust earthquake is nothing to balk at. Was the most powerful in U.S. history and it killed over a hundred people and sent tsunamis that demolished villages. Did you know it was the second worst recorded earthquake in the history of the world?"

She noticed the wonder on his face. "And you're telling me that quake wasn't a big one?"

"It was decent. But nothing earth shattering. Alaska has the most active seismic activity of all fifty US states. During the last century, we've had nine out of the ten biggest earthquakes in the US. It has more earthquakes than any state in the nation and is one of the most seismically active regions in the world."

"Didn't know that." Hatch wasn't sure how much she'd recall from the conversation, but at least it gave her a break from the situation they were heading toward.

"You and your friends picked a hell of a time to come to Breakneck. Wendy's mighty pissed off."

"Nothing like a woman scorned." Hatch smiled at her comment. "If that wasn't the big one, then when? Where?"

"Honest opinion? It's hard to tell. If anyone could predict it, people would evacuate beforehand. There's science, and then there's quake whispering." Hatch gave him a look. He smiled. "It's what I call it, and I don't really whisper to the quakes. I listen."

"And that's how you knew where to park so you didn't fall in the sinkhole?"

Hill laughed hard and slapped the wheel. "My goodness, no. That was pure coincidence. I wasn't listening to the ground. I was checking Jessie's undercarriage. There was a loud clanging sound. Haven't heard anything since we've been driving, so I guess it's fixed itself. Maybe Wendy's little temper tantrum shook whatever needed fixing back into place. She tends to do that."

"Do what?" Hatch wondered what had been the cause of the sound that had sent Hill under the van to investigate. Would it crop up again when they were off road?

"Help. She gave me purpose. Sure, she redirected my life at an early age, but I've made peace with that long ago. Now, I see the purpose in what I do, even if nobody else does."

"How much time until the next one? I know geologically speaking the big one is coming 'soon'. That could be thousands of years, though. What do you think?"

Hill swung his head side to side. Jessie followed. "If I knew that, I'd be a millionaire. And probably wouldn't be driving toward it."

"What do you mean 'driving toward it'?"

"I mean that every bit of data I've crunched since the '64 quake has led me to believe the big one is coming soon. And all signs are pointing to Breakneck as the epicenter." Hill then gripped the steering wheel tightly, whitening his knuckles. "Hang tight, we're about to go off road."

Hill drove with the same reckless abandon he'd shown on the paved road. Somehow, he managed to navigate the trail's slick, muddy surface without losing control. Jessie fishtailed as they rounded a bend. "How far up is that thing saying we have to go?" His voice strained as if *he* were traversing the steady incline. The rain turned into ice, cutting visibility to less than five feet ahead. It sounded like nails bouncing off the hood and windshield.

Hatch checked their location. "Looks like once we get around that bend in the trail, we'll have less than a quarter-mile to go until we reach our objective."

"I hear the military in the way you talk. I don't see a uniform or badge, so I'm guessing you and your friends are some type of government contractors. Am I close?"

Close? He was spot on. But Hatch felt it better not to add credence to his claim. "You know the old saying, if you have to ask—"

"I probably don't need to know." He offered an apologetic smile. "I get it. Not trying to be nosy. Just wondering if your team being here has anything to do with that kidnapped deputy marshal."

She measured her words, careful to reveal little. "It does. Though, I'm here as an observer."

Hill eyed her and gave a shake of his head. "Doesn't look that way to me."

Hatch dropped the conversation and Hill made no attempt to pick it back up again. Jessie rounded the bend. Hill kept her speed up to compensate for the steady incline. The tires no longer had traction. Worse, the precipitation had reached whiteout conditions, further restricting visibility, making it almost impossible to see the roadblock that appeared out of nowhere. Through a curtain of sleet, Hatch spotted the seventy-foot Douglas Fir, uprooted and laying across the trail.

EIGHTEEN

HILL WHIPPED THE STEERING WHEEL TO AVOID THE ROADBLOCK. THE van fishtailed. Jessie did her best to do as Hill commanded, but conditions dictated otherwise. A loud bang rang out, and Hatch felt the front passenger side dip down.

The van had barely managed the treacherous terrain with four wheels and was now losing control. Jessie spun as the front right wheel well dug into the soft earth as it spun. A flat tire brought them to an abrupt halt and left them facing in the opposite direction.

"Looks like we're walking." Hill threw the van into park and looked over at Hatch.

"You've come far enough." She placed her hand on his wrist. "I can't ask you to risk more than you have."

"You didn't ask. And this isn't up for a debate. I told you I was in. And when I'm in, I'm all in."

"You're speaking my language." Hatch opened the door to a blast of ice pellets. "Now, let's go get my friend before Wendy gets any other ideas."

Hill stopped and got on all fours, just like he had done when inspecting Jessie's undercarriage moments before the quake that swallowed half the road and nearly killed them while they were parked in front of Old Man Gentry's place. He put his ear close to the ground with the flap, protecting it from touching the ice-coated mud. He closed his eyes and nodded to himself. Hill stood a moment later. He dusted a fresh layer of wet snow from his flight jacket and gave a thumbs up. "Good to go. At least for the time being. Wendy's quiet, but I'm not sure for how long."

"Thought you said you didn't listen to the ground?"

He patted the wet mud with his hand. "I listen when she talks. Chivalry is not dead with me. Truth be known, me and this ole' girl go way back. Wendy's the yin to my yang. That doesn't mean she can't have her bad days. Like in '64. In the years since Wendy took my mother's life, I have come to look at it differently. We can't control the earth and sky. They don't belong to us. Even if they did, they've got a mind of their own. The titans of old awaken from time to time to remind us how truly small and insignificant we really are."

Hatch thought of the powerful hold her father's death had on her, and the cataclysmic fallout from her exposure to the truth. "Doesn't mean we lay down and die."

"Never crossed my mind. I fight tooth and nail with Wendy. Have been my whole life. And as you've seen, she's got a hell of a temper."

"Then let's try not to piss her off."

Soft mud hardened underfoot. Each step forward was a step up as they set out in the direction of Cruise and his team. As the distance between them and the van increased, the precipitation lightened until it was nothing more than a flurry.

Hatch shook off the cold. Her jacket had done a decent job repelling the water. A nifty button she found on the inside of her right sleeve had three wavy lines. She pressed it and within minutes she was not only warm, but dry. Not much she could do about her lower extremities, but a little creature comfort went a long way on the battlefield. And she was definitely on a battlefield.

The trail snaked back around to the right and up ahead was the Land Rover. Hatch understood why Cruise hadn't been able to give status on Hertzog when he'd messaged. A massive boulder had sheared the SUV in two.

Hertzog's enormous torso hung halfway out of the Land Rover's rear window. A large chunk of glass was sticking out of Hertzog's left forearm. He'd lost a lot of blood, as evidenced by the dark pool formed beneath him.

"He's alive." Hatch pressed against Hertzog's thick neck and located a faint pulse.

"Hardheaded, I guess." Hill stood beside Hatch.

"He's not out of the woods yet. That glass is in deep. We're going to have to pack it and wrap it tight before we move." Hatch dipped her head into the rear compartment. It was barely recognizable. She thought of Cruise's message, *I'm pinned*. Hatch pushed her worry from her mind. Battlefield triage was necessary. Hertzog was first up, and she deemed his situation critical. Hatch held a small med kit in her hand. "Got any more of that Baywatch rescue in you?"

Hill tipped his trapper cap and took the med kit from Hatch. "He's in good hands."

Hatch was already on the move. Rounding the boulder, more of the landslide's destruction confronted her. Outside the demolished front end of the Land Rover was Brady Taylor. His body was twisted into an unnatural position. The light orange of Taylor's hair was darkened with his blood. His neck was turned one-hundred and eighty degrees. Hatch never assumed and pressed her fingers alongside his neck. Cold to the touch. No pulse.

Taylor stared up at her with lifeless eyes. She was back in Afghanistan looking at her ginger-haired teammate and best friend, Graham Benson, who'd been killed by a suicide bomber during an ambush. One fraction of a second hesitation detoured Hatch's path in life and branded her in the snarled branches of scar tissue.

"Rach?" Cruise's voice was weak, and barely travelled beyond his confines. He was fighting for consciousness in the prison of jagged steel that used to be the front passenger compartment. Hatch peered in through the driver's side. Cruise's upper body stretched across the center console and onto the driver's seat. His lower extremities were pinned by the folded passenger side door. He was trapped.

The same metal tubing used to reinforce the Land Rover, which saved Cruise's life, was now working hard to take it. A thick steel rod running horizontal along the center of the door bent inward, and the point of it penetrated deep into Cruise's upper right thigh.

"Hang on." Hatch yanked hard at the driver's side door. It opened a few inches and then stopped. Hatch gripped the door's frame along the window. She arched back, pulling with all her might. The door dug into her fingers, but wouldn't budge beyond its initial movement.

The snapped branch of a Black Spruce lay across the hood. Hatch grabbed it. She made eye contact with Hill, who was still on the other side of the boulder at the severed back end tending to Hertzog. He had managed to get Hertzog out and onto the ground. Hill knelt beside the unconscious Talon operator and gave a bloody thumbs up.

He shouted over the howling wind. "I've got the wound packed. Tourniquet is set. But he's got to get to a hospital soon or none of it is gonna matter."

"That's the plan. FBI will be arriving at the landing zone soon. I want to be there to greet them when they do. I'll need your help once I get this door open, but in the meantime, think you can grab some of those boards from your van and rig something together so we can haul our load?"

"Consider it done." Hill jogged off, heading down the muddy trail toward the van.

Hatch slid the branch between the gap in the door and the frame of the SUV's b-pillar. Loud crunching and popping sounded as she worked the piece of timber back and forth. After putting up an exhausting fight, the door yielded to Hatch's relentless effort and opened.

Cruise looked up at her. His eyes glossy and distant. The brightness of the cobalt was all but gone. She bent in. Her face hovered over his. "I'm going to get you out of here. Understand?"

He blinked. His lips were moving, but no sound reached Hatch. She leaned in close. His breath tickled her ear. His words came in short inconsistent bursts. "I want...you...to meet me...where...the... moon meets...the sea."

Hatch felt a pang in her heart. "Hang tight. We've got helos inbound. I'm going to get you out of here."

"Promise me." His voice just above a whisper. "I lost you once. Not again." Each blink was slower and more pronounced than its predecessor. And with each blink, Cruise's eyes remained closed longer and longer.

Hatch pressed her lips against his. She was met by the cold flesh of the man she'd once planned to marry. He spoke again. This time there was no sound. Hatch felt the word through vibration of lips. *Promise.*

"Promise."

The clacking of wood alerted Hatch to Hill's clamorous approach. He had three wood planks lashed together by the cargo net used to hold back the paint cans. A rope was secured to it as a harness. "Should be wide enough. And with you and me pullin' together, should be doable."

"Was there another tourniquet in that med kit?"

"No. I can rummage around and see what I can find."

"No time." Hatch snapped a smaller branch from one she'd used to pry the door. "Bring me that roll of gauze."

Hatch climbed inside. She bound Cruise's leg above the wound using the long strip of sterile bandage provided by Hill. Hatch's hands were slick with blood as she slid the six-inch branch under the knot. Hatch turned it to the right until the resistance was too great. She then locked it into place. Using her bloody finger as a pen, Hatch marked a T on Cruise's forehead, making a note of the time underneath.

"This is going to hurt like hell. But it's the only way."

Cruise blinked once and then closed his eyes. The color continued to drain from his face.

Hatch then turned to Hill. "We're losing him. On three we're going to pull him free."

Hatch gripped Cruise by the left arm. Hill took up the right. The two worked together to yank Cruise clear of the metal pinning him. Cruise's eyes never reopened, despite what must have been agonizing pain as his leg ripped free.

The two then worked fast to get all three Talon men, including the deceased Taylor, aboard the makeshift sled. Hill ran a rope around the three men, securing them to the boards like a seat belt.

"What about all that gear? Don't want to be leavin' it out here for those white supremacist assholes to find."

Hatch looked around, desperate for a way. "No way we can make good time with all that extra weight. Once we get them to the chopper, I'll come back for it."

"*We'll* come back for it." Hill gave a wink and then took up his end of the rope.

The sound of a helicopter could be heard just above the wind. Renewed with the hope of salvation nearby, Hatch and Hill led the sled away from the wreckage and began making the mile long trek toward the landing zone.

NINETEEN

AN ARDUOUS THIRTY MINUTES LATER, HATCH AND HILL BROUGHT Cruise and team to the landing zone, a plateau east of the glacier. Members of the FBI's Hostage Rescue Team rushed toward them. Hatch was surprised to see one of the operators was a female.

The woman introduced herself as Agent Babiarz and her partner as Medina. They then assisted with the sled.

"Where's the medical chopper?" Hatch asked.

"Tied up. It's a real shit show everywhere right now." Babiarz locked eyes with Hatch as she took the rope from her. Medina swapped out Hill's end. Fresh legs picked up the final sprint to the finish. "But one of our guys is a fully trained paramedic. They'll be in good hands. Can't guarantee anything, but our guy will do his best."

Hatch jogged alongside. She looked down at the three men being carted in Hill's sled. Their bodies shook as they rumbled across the flatland toward the awaiting helicopters.

"What are we looking at?" An HRT operator by the name of Wren greeted Hatch and Babiarz under the rotating blades of the first chopper.

"One dead. Two critical." Hatch shouted over the *whomp-whomp* of the rotors, never looking up from Cruise. She squeezed his hand and willed him to hold on.

"Put the two critical on chopper one with me." Wren set out three backboards on the wet ground beside the sled.

Hill undid the bindings. He moved Taylor's corpse out of the way, transferring him to the furthest gurney while the others worked on moving the other two. Wren and Medina strained while moving Hertzog.

Hatch gripped Cruise at his boots while Babiarz took his shoulders. They hoisted him up and over to the stretcher board in one smooth motion. Wren finished strapping in Hertzog and made his way over.

Hatch looked down at Cruise's combat boot and tried not to allow her mind to wander to all the battlefield crosses she'd seen over the years. She focused on the six uniquely designed whisper-quiet retractable crampon claws inlaid within the bottom of its sole. Cruise was her height. And looked to be about her boot size, give or take half an inch.

Wren made the final adjustments to the straps and then went back to Hertzog. Wren and Medina hustled as fast as they could to manage Hertzog's dead weight. Hatch removed Cruise's bloodstained boots and set them beside her.

"What are you doing with those?" Babiarz asked.

Hatch sat on the wet ground beside Cruise and took her boots off. She stood back up after completing the footwear swap. "I'm going back."

"The hell you are!" Hatch turned to see an imposing man with steel eyes and the weathered look of a seasoned operator. "You and your team had your chance. Time to let us get it done. Should've been ours to begin with."

"Who are you?"

"Cal Roe."

"So?"

"I'm HRT Commander."

"Where's the assault team?" Hatch asked.

"On standby in Anchorage." Roe was fuming.

"Anchorage? It's going to take your team over an hour to get here."

"Two. We still have to fly back and refuel." Roe eyed the chopper Cruise and Hertzog were being loaded into. "Hell, that's if we get the green light. After this fiasco and the unstable ground situation, who knows how long that'll be."

"Thank you for making my case." Hatch walked closer to Cruise. She removed the Kimber Custom II semiautomatic pistol from the dropdown holster on his right leg.

"Don't even think about it." Roe stepped in Hatch's path. "I already spoke with Tracy."

"I don't work for Talon." Hatch stepped around Roe.

"Who the hell are you?"

"Hatch."

"And you think you're just going to walk in and save Lawson all by yourself? With nothing but a pistol?" He laughed. "Damn crazy woman."

"There's more gear in their SUV." Hatch tucked the pistol at the small of her back and then jogged off. "And who said anything about walking?"

Roe crossed his arms over his chest and shook his head. "The next time these choppers come back, it's gonna be with my assault team. You understand me? There will be no rescue mission for you. We will not be returning for you."

Hatch ignored Roe's threat and picked up the pace of her jog. She slowed when Burton Hill ran up alongside her on the left. "Where to next, partner?"

"Sorry, this next part I do alone."

Hill looked hurt. "I could be an extra set of eyes. A lookout, ya know. I keep watch and you do whatever Greatest American Hero thing you do."

"Those men on that chopper owe you for saving their lives. And I owe you for all you've done. But I will not repay that debt by sending you to your grave." She stopped and faced him. "Mind if I borrow your keys?"

Hill stared at her for a minute without speaking as he processed what she was asking. His lips drew tight, and he began nodding.

"Spare is on the back." Hill handed the keys over. "Take care of her for me."

"I'll have Jessie back in one piece."

Hill slowed and dropped back. "Fair winds and following seas."

A loud crack like that of a bullwhip the length of the Mississippi River filled the air. Hatch was thrown into the air and landed on the wet ground. She regained her footing and looked back. A twenty-foot divide now separated Hatch from the others. She looked on without any way to assist as a helicopter fell into the void.

TWENTY

Flames sent black smoke billowing out of the helicopter's tail. A massive spruce, upended along the opposite side of the newly formed ridge line, dipped low into the divide. The tail rotor got caught up in the tree's branches. Hundred-year-old roots gave the tree enough strength to hold the helicopter, at least for the time being.

On the ground, Babz collected herself. The quake had thrown rock and debris everywhere, and it took her a moment to make heads or tails of the world. A trickle of blood under her eye warmed her right cheek.

As her teammates were taking stock of themselves, Babz looked around to see who was missing. The two injured, Cruise and Hertzog, were still safe within the helicopter. Wren gave a thumbs up.

The shriek of twisting metal rang out. Babz spun. The other Blackhawk, the one containing Hoop and the body of the deceased Taylor, was hanging off the edge of a newly formed chasm. Without a moment's hesitation, Babz jumped up and raced into action.

Babz grimaced at the sting in her leg. She looked down and saw a thin shard of metal sticking out below her knee. She detached herself from the pain and focused on the fact that it looked like a drinking straw. Reaching down, she yanked it out. The warm blood rolling down her leg and into her boot made her pulse pound louder, but she pressed on.

She skidded to a stop when she came to the edge of the crash site. What was she dealing with here? She edged herself closer to the helicopter. The bird was hung up between the branches of the broken tree and the deep, gnarled roots that were still holding it all together. Splintered wood reached out over the crevasse like a giant arm cradling a crushed toy. The mangled remains of the helicopter pointed nose down into the dark hole. From Babz's current position, she saw no signs of life. An arm hung loosely from the side of the chopper's open door. Working her way to the helicopter, she checked it first to see if it could carry any weight at all.

The tail was closest to her. With any luck, she could rappel down it to get a closer look inside. But as she tested the tail to see if her weight would cause the helicopter to tumble, the smoking metal groaned. It was too dangerous to work her way down the helicopter. She'd have to navigate the jagged bits of rock and debris. She was grateful that the ground was still cold enough to stay firm and not break apart in her hands. She climbed down until her body was parallel with the open side door and peered inside. There was movement.

Relief washed over her. "Can any of you climb out?"

The pilot unbuckled himself and then reached forward. As he put weight on his ankle, he screamed out loud. The bone was snapped. He fell into the cockpit area and slammed into the instrument panel. The helicopter shifted. The latch holding the stretcher released, and Taylor's body shot forward and out through the broken front windshield. The ginger haired Talon operator disappeared into the blackness below.

"Shit!" Wren yelled.

Hoop had been riding co-pilot. His body hung limp, his arms dangling forward toward the shattered front windshield. He remained unresponsive.

"Hoop!" Babz called out.

"Ah." Grunting and groaning,

"He's still with us," Babz relayed.

"Tough son of a bitch," Medina said as he came up alongside Babz.

"I got him," the pilot said.

"No, you don't. You need to get out."

"I can't leave him."

"Get yourself out. I'll take care of Hoop. Can you climb up?" She could see the pilot wanted to argue the point further, but when he looked down at his shattered, unnaturally twisted ankle, he let the words fall silent and crawled forward. He made slow but steady progress up, working himself to the skid plate and over to the jagged ground. The exposed tree roots served as a makeshift ladder. Babz outstretched her hand. She and Medina hung over the cliff's face and pulled the pilot up the rest of the way.

Medina and Wren immediately went to work on triaging the pilot's injuries. The damage from the fall went far beyond the ankle to include broken ribs, head wounds, lacerations. The stench of blood and scorched flesh was overwhelming.

Medina had a laceration around the back of his left ear that painted the whole side of his neck red. His hand gripped Babz's forearm tightly. "You sure you don't need my help?"

Babz managed a smirk. " I need you to get your ass patched up and trust me that I can bring Hoop out."

"I will." He reached past her, but stopped. "And I do."

Medina climbed out as Babz climbed in. She worked her way down, easing to the front of the aircraft. A loud creak sounded. She heard the crack of wood splintering. Babz braced herself, grabbing onto a loose cargo strap as the chopper dropped about seven feet before catching on another root. Her stomach was in her throat until the momentum stopped. Not wasting a second, Babz worked herself toward the cockpit, trying not to think about the other creaks and groans growing around her.

She finally reached Hoop. He was still unconscious. A trickle of blood was coming out of his left ear, leading her to believe he must've banged his head. She couldn't see any other sign of injury, but there was no rousing him. No, she had to do this all on her own. She gave the seatbelt a try. It didn't budge. Knowing each precious second counted, Babz pulled out her knife and cut through it.

Next, she worked his body onto hers like a sloppy rucksack. She almost buckled under his dead weight. Digging deep, she clung to the adrenalin still surging through her veins. Babz hoisted the massive commander into place. Then, taking a line of parachute cord peeking out from one of the gear bags, she lashed it around them both, cinching it tight so that it bit under her armpits and pulled tightly under his, securing his torso to hers.

As she crawled forward bit by bit, she felt every ounce of his two-hundred-thirty-seven-pound frame. She willed the riotous noise of the teetering chopper to stop. She focused only on getting out alive. Babz concentrated on the steady sound of her breath. In for one, out for two. In for one, out for two.

Keep moving forward and you'll eventually get there.

She heard it again, her father's voice, like he was there with her. It was almost as if she felt his strength as her boot pressed hard against the skid pad. A loud creak sounded and broke her concentration and forced her to look up. The root no longer held. The earthy arm holding the helicopter had given up its fight against the call of the crevasse's deep and unending darkness, and it pulled like a vortex.

Babz launched forward with all her might. She shot herself into the jagged rocky face of the cliff. Her grip waned, and she slipped down until her fingers grazed a hold and latched on. She held on and pressed her body tight to the cliff face until she had caught her breath. Then she began the arduous task of ascending the next twenty feet, one hand, then one foot at a time, all while carrying Hoop.

Her movements grew sluggish as adrenalin ebbed, and she felt the full weight of gravity working against her. Babz got her right hand atop the ledge. Her fingers sunk into slushy ice, but there was nowhere for her to get a grip. Hoop's weight started tugging her back toward the darkness, toward the emptiness where the helicopter had fallen.

The crash that echoed up to her when it hit bottom was very far off, leaving no room for doubt. There would be no chance of survival if she didn't make it over the ledge. She tried to push failure from her mind, but now instead of her breath, she felt her heartbeat's rapid rhythm take over.

Her hands started slipping. She dug her fingernails into the ground, clawing at the solid earth. She could feel the dirt tearing her nails from her flesh. Babz held fast through the pain, until suddenly it was alleviated by Medina's firm grip. With the other team members anchored behind him, they pulled Babz and Hoop the rest of the way out.

She collapsed on solid ground with her face buried in snow and exhaled for the first time in several minutes. The team quickly unhooked Hoop from her and transported him over to the one working helicopter, now a sea of wounded. Radio communications had gone out and several ambulances were on their way. Temporary first aid was being given to the members that needed it most until the paramedics arrived. Exhausted, Babz climbed to her feet and dusted herself off. Medina's bright grin waited for her.

"Glad you made it."

"Was there ever any doubt?" she shot back, returning his smile.

Medina clapped her on the back. "With you? Never."

Babz thanked Medina, who went off to help the others while she caught her breath. She was still trying to wrap her mind around what just happened when movement caught her eye.

Babz looked across the gap. Hatch stood on the opposite side. Their eyes locked for a long moment. Hatch gave Babz a nod of her head before turning and disappearing deeper into the wooded area beneath the ice cap.

Babz continued to stare into the tree line, wondering if Hatch would return. She lingered a moment longer before she dusted herself off and went back to her teammates, her head held a bit higher.

TWENTY-ONE

IT WAS AS IF SOMEBODY TOOK A GIANT ERASER AND DRAGGED IT ACROSS the ATV trail where the Talon Land Rover had been. Broken bits of plastic, metal, and glass were littered across the ice-covered muddy path, crumbs leftover after the earth swallowed both halves of the severed SUV and most of the boulder. Hatch deduced the last quake had further shifted the already unstable ground where the landslide had occurred.

Hatch looked at the naturally formed gravestone and cursed under her breath. The gear, including the MK34 White Phosphorus grenades, was now submerged under tons of dirt and rock. It'd take an excavator to access it or a week for Hatch to dig it out by hand. Neither option was viable. Hatch jogged around the bend. Jessie was still there. She felt the keys of Hill's beloved van. Her extract vehicle was still above ground, flat tire or not.

Carrying on, Hatch used the first weapon her father had trained her to use. Her body. Her legs.

Be the vehicle of your own mission, her father's lesson after they'd run the trail behind her childhood home in Hawk's Landing. She was young, maybe ten at the time, but Hatch heard the words as clear as she had that day.

The lesson was a simple, but hard one. He'd pushed her further that day than he ever had before. Her father took her on a trail three miles out at an exhausting pace. She fought to keep up. When they'd reached the turnaround point, he looked at her and smiled. "Don't be late for dinner." He took off running back the way they'd come at a faster pace than their initial one. Hatch lost sight of her father within a quarter mile.

Winded and physically spent, Hatch had to find a pace that enabled her to beat the dinner clock. In the remaining two-plus miles, she found a sustainable rhythm.

She also learned a second lesson that day. It came to her later and after several days of being angry at her dad for leaving her alone to find her way home. He finally confronted her and asked why she was still mad.

Hatch had said, "You left me!" She remembered how he laughed at her comment. It only served to anger her further then. But now, how she missed that laugh. It was as rare as a unicorn, but when it appeared, it was pure magic. Then he said something that she carried with her through the darkest time.

I left you so you would understand how strong you are. Every time you feel tired, and you can't go on, remember that day on the trail. Remember that you took your body beyond where your mind would allow. I was with you all along, even when you couldn't see me. There will be times where you'll be alone and afraid. Remember this day. Remember I was there. Know I always will be.

Hatch inhaled the frigid Alaskan air. The muscle fibers in her thighs and calves tingled. Her father was with her, here and now, as she stood where Talon's mission ended and hers began. She could not fail. He would not let her.

She made quick work getting to the base of the glacier. She stopped before the ground shifted to pure ice just beyond the tree line. This was unfamiliar territory for her. She'd seen a few documentaries but had minimal training when it came to traversing a glacier. She pressed the button on the side of each boot and the claws extended from the bottom.

Metal teeth bit hard into the ice with each step. At sixty-nine hundred feet elevation, she felt the exertion. Each breath she took made her lungs burn. Every step resulted in fire in her legs. She shrouded her face as best she could from the onslaught of sub-zero temperatures made worse by the whipping wind. The hood on the jacket provided by Talon Executive Services did its part, keeping her warm, while the crampon boots of Cruise enabled her to maintain a steady pace along the icy terrain.

Hatch had to step carefully. The cloud-shrouded moon gave just enough reflection for her to navigate the more obvious dips and tears in the ground's surface, but the smaller ones were harder to see and the white on white made it difficult to see the crevasses before she was upon them.

She pulled out her cell phone and checked again. There hadn't been a signal since the last quake. Hatch had no contact with the outside world. She was alone. But so was Lawson, and Hatch wasn't planning on letting him die that way. She considered using the flashlight on the phone to help her navigate the treacherous landscape. But she decided against it, as the light could give her position away.

The wind masked most of the noise made by her movement across the ice. She had expected there to be loud crunching. Cruise had been right; the unique design of the boot claws enabled her to maintain noise discipline while on the run.

As she came over the ridge of ice, the campground came into view. Hatch paused to take in the scene. There was no movement outside of the cafeteria. Light penetrated the covered windows but provided no visibility into the building's interior. She had a mental picture of the layout and the last thermal image of Lawson's position. Reaching the location would not be easy. Without a team of operators and armed only with Cruise's pistol, Hatch prepared to finish what Talon started.

Thirty feet away from the side door to the cafeteria, Hatch stopped and stood still. Above the wind and generator rose the roar of an engine. Different from a car or truck, the approaching vehicles sounded more like an amplified lawnmower. Cones of light pierced the darkness. Hatch sought the only refuge from view available.

A Pippin & Son Port-A-John was about ten feet from her on the left. Hatch darted behind it. She held the .45 caliber Kimber in her left hand while she waited. It wasn't long before two ATVs skidded to a stop. The ground crunched underneath.

In the porch light, Hatch spotted Frank Winslow. She recalled his face from the dossier. The other man remained straddled across his ATV a moment longer. Hatch recognized this man even though darkness cast him in shadow. He was impossible to miss. The enormous six-foot-nine behemoth, Walter Grizzly, rose like a mountain that dominated the skyline. He dipped his head back and sniffed the air, then scanned his surroundings before entering the cafeteria.

Hatch had seen two enemies. That left Buck Mathers, Sam Kirkland, Todd Lankowski, and Chris MacIntosh unaccounted for. And then there was Lawson. Hatch hoped she wasn't already too late.

She remained motionless behind the outhouse for a full minute. Nobody else entered or exited the building. She prepared to move toward the side door when she heard a low whimper reverberating through the faded green plastic of the portable bathroom she was standing behind.

She moved fast, exposing herself as she stepped around to the front and ripped open the door to the Port-A-John. Hatch looked down the front sight at Lankowski. Wide-eyed, he stared back. He squirmed, but the ropes binding his wrists and ankles together hindered his movement. The gag around his mouth muffled his attempts to scream as Hatch stepped inside.

TWENTY-TWO

BLOOD LEAKED FROM LANKOWSKI'S BROKEN NOSE DOWN THE CONTOURS of his face where it collected on the torn cloth gagging his mouth. The cop killer whimpered as he twisted against his bindings. All his efforts only worked to tighten them, digging deeper into his flesh.

Hatch stared at him with indifference. She would have been happy to knock him around and shove his head into the piss-filled water tank. But he had knowledge she needed. Would he talk? Only one way to find out. She aimed the pistol at his forehead and waited for his whimpering to die down.

"You and I are going to have a little talk." Hatch kept her voice at a whisper. "You will speak only when I tell you to and you will not try calling for help, or I will spread your brains all over this shitter. Got that? That gag comes off, I ask the questions and you answer. Simple as that. Think you can handle it?"

His eyes darted wildly as he considered the terms and eventually nodded. She undid the gag. The second the cloth was removed, Lankowski opened his mouth to scream. The first syllable never left his lips. Hatch struck down hard with the butt end of Cruise's Kimber. The bottom of the magazine hit bullseye, striking his broken nose.

Fresh blood spurted from a laceration running across the bridge of Lankowski's nose. He clenched his eyes tight. His mouth twisted open, and he choked on his sobs.

Hatch brought the pistol up, just as she'd done before. "That one was a warning."

After a bout of hyperventilating, Lankowski regained some measure of composure. "Who the hell are you, lady?"

"Who I am doesn't matter. What I tell you to do and you complying with it is the only thing that does. If you answer me honestly and make no more pathetic attempts to cry for help, then you *may* get out of this alive."

He stared up at Hatch and tried to spit blood. It dribbled over his bottom lip and trickled down his chin. The defiance he'd shown a moment ago was all but gone. Lankowski lowered his head and slumped his shoulders in defeat.

"Where's Lawson?"

"Lady, you're in way over your head." Lankowski's forehead wrinkled as he eyed Hatch. "When's the rest of the cavalry arriving?"

"Why don't you worry less about me and more about what you need to do and say to not die on a crapper?"

"You're on your own." He laughed. Wind rattled the green plastic walls of the outhouse, forcing Lankowski to raise his voice. "That's it. It's just you all by your lonesome."

"By the looks of your face and those ropes around your wrists and ankles, I'd say I'm not alone."

"Grizz and the boys are gonna have a good time with you." Lankowski made a slow and deliberate pass of his tongue over his blood-caked lips. "Hope they save me a piece."

"You're as useless as you look." Hatch pulled the gag back into place.

Lankowski's words transitioned into a whimper. She brought the pistol butt down over his head one more time for good measure. He slumped back against the rear wall.

Hatch turned in the tight space. She peeked out at the cafeteria through a gap in the door. Light flickered from inside. The windows had all been covered in newspaper, but she saw the shadows of three men through them. She made one last visual sweep of the icy landscape before exiting. She unlatched the door and stepped out onto the ice when she was struck from behind.

Lankowski had launched himself out of the port-a-john. With his hands and feet bound, he made an armless tackle. His body collided with Hatch's right side. The claws of her boots locked her leg in place at the point of impact. Her ankle rolled inward. She fought back a scream at the pain.

She tossed Lankowski aside. He stumbled a few steps, then went face first into ice-covered gravel. Hatch straightened her ankle. A fireball shot up the right side of her body, pulsing from her ankle to her hip with every beat of her heart. She breathed deeply, trying to control the pain. *In for four. Out for four.* Hatch repeated the box-breathing exercise until she pushed the pain out of her mind.

She regained her footing and turned to face Lankowski. He wriggled backward across the ice like a legless lizard stuck on its back. The wind doused his whimpered cries for help.

Lankowski made a weak attempt to kick at her as Hatch grabbed him by the rope tied at the ankles. The slick ground made it easy for her to drag him back to the outhouse. She dropped his legs, moved around to the other side of him, and hooked her arms under his. Once she had him in a squatting position, she shoved him inside with no regard to where he landed. Lankowski lay on the urine-stained floor of the Port-A-John. He stared at Hatch with bloodshot eyes as he grunted his protest through the gag in his mouth.

Hatch weighed her options. Her swollen ankle pressed against the inside of the boot. She knelt and retied the boot, pulling the laces as taut as she could manage. Speed was her advantage in this and most situations. Lankowski's stunt took that away. Hatch tucked the Kimber in her waist and retrieved a folding knife from an inside zippered pocket on her coat.

"I gave you one warning. Just one. And your dumbass failed to heed it." Hatch opened the blade. Lankowski's eyes went wide. "You wanted to be a hero and warn your friends. Well, I'm going to give you an opportunity to do just that. In fact, I'm going to need you to scream."

Hatch slammed the blade into the gunshot wound on Lankowski's foot. She then used the same knife to cut the gag free. As Lankowski's screams cut through the howling wind, Hatch set off toward the side entrance of the cafeteria as quickly as her injured ankle would allow.

TWENTY-THREE

THE LIGHT FROM ABOVE FLICKERED ON AND OFF, OR IT AT LEAST appeared to. Lawson lay flat on his back. He had no way to account for the passage of time. He had been in and out of consciousness the entire time. Could've been an hour. Could've been a week. He had no idea. He recalled the past day of his life in bite-sized chunks, like binge watching a series but only getting to see select scenes. Four of them replayed in Lawson's mind on a perpetual loop every time his eyes closed, which was happening more frequently now, and for longer periods of time. The ability to open his eyes again took more and more effort. He feared the point was fast approaching where they would not open again. Worse, he began to welcome that moment.

As the back of his eyelids became the movie screen, the looped cycle of recent memory began its replay from the beginning. It started with the fight with his wife, one that never would have happened if he had only listened to her wants and needs. Then the gunfight that left his partner Hicks, a father of seven, dead. He saw everything they did wrong. It shouldn't have gone down that way. Next came the severing of his right ear. The camera had been turned on him and he witnessed it in excruciating detail. And lastly, the belt buckle beating. He found it strange that all hope rested with an ex-con who'd not only saved him from certain death at the hands of Lankowski, but then went on to tend to his wounds.

MacIntosh didn't speak as he set about his task. Not that Lawson could offer much in the way of conversation even if he had. Ever since receiving the blow from the belt buckle, and having a bandage wrapped tightly around it, Lawson hadn't been able to move his jaw. The sting had subsided, and now was nothing more than a tingle.

Lawson had little feeling anywhere in his body now, just enough to feel the vibration rolling across the floorboards. Lawson knew this was no quake. He wished it was, though, because this was something much worse.

"What the hell happened in here?" Grizzly's voice boomed as he slammed something against the floor.

Lawson caught a glimpse of the enormous man, his stature more amplified from Lawson's supine position.

"Lank," MacIntosh muttered. "That boy went wild. Bashed Lawson's face in with that stupid belt buckle of his."

That comment earned a chuckle from Winslow.

MacIntosh continued. "He would've killed him if I didn't jump in."

Grizzly moved closer. He now stood directly beneath the hole in the ceiling from the single shot fired during MacIntosh's struggle with Lank. "Is he still alive?"

"Hanging on by a thread. You understand that means our window of opportunity to get the hell off this ice cube is quickly closing."

"Don't matter anyway. The proof of life was never sent." Winslow was pacing behind Grizzly. Both sides of his mismatched face bore the same murderous rage. "Never seen nothin' like it in my entire life. One minute Buck was taking Deputy Dipshit's ear to the camp's welcome sign, the next they're gone."

It felt as though the air had been sucked out of the room.

"Gone?" MacIntosh was standing somewhere close on the left side but out of view.

"I mean G-O-N-E gone. Friggin' ice just split. Didn't ever hear them scream. Never heard them hit the bottom."

"We're down two." Grizzly's voice rumbled like Harley on the open road. "Ain't gonna be draggin' this piece of shit around with us. Time to cut our losses."

MacIntosh offered a protest. "I thought you agreed he's worth more to us alive than dead."

"Change of plans. He's dead weight." Grizzly looked around the room. "Speaking of dead weight, where's Lank?"

"Got pissed off after I put a stop to his bullshit." MacIntosh was a good liar. The words rolled off his tongue as though he weren't concocting the story on the fly. "Probably went off to get high. Damn junkie."

A low growl rumbled from the throat of the giant as he glanced around the room, noting the extent of the struggle that had occurred there.

"Listen," MacIntosh said. "I've already got my ATV ready to strap him in. He won't slow me down. If he dies, I'll dump him. To do so sooner would be idiotic. Might as well use him while we can. I'll shoulder the burden." MacIntosh was once again serving as Lawson's defense council.

Grizz narrowed his eyes at the man. "You seem to have taken a real shine to our law dog."

"Not at all. I'd prefer to put a bullet in his head, but like I said before, keeping him alive might be the only reason this compound isn't flooded with federal agents. You can be sure they're coming, though."

"You don't need leverage in war. You need violence. I'm real good at violence. The boys ever tell you how I earned my mark?" Grizz allowed no time for MacIntosh to respond. "Choked the life right out of the guy with my bare hands. I felt the crunch of his neck when I snapped it."

"What'd he do to deserve it?"

"Cheated me in a poker game." Grizz shrugged.

"Tell him the best part." Winslow popped into view.

"Turns out the little douchebag didn't cheat. He'd played a fair hand. I was high as a kite. I guess I got things confused. It was the other kid at the table who'd been cheating." Smile lines formed and Grizz offered a shrug. "Mistakes happen. But I clean up after myself.

That little shit, the one who'd cheated, tried to protect himself by turning state's witness for the case. They still haven't found him. Mathers and Kirkland ain't the first two people I've seen disappear into a crevasse."

MacIntosh squared up to Grizz. "Please don't tell me your plan is to choke a swarm of heavily armed and well-trained federal agents?"

Grizz did not laugh. Lawson felt the vibration as Grizz stepped forward. The two men were chest to chin. "You best not be pokin' the bear, boy."

"Not trying to." MacIntosh went back into defense council mode. "I'm not afraid of dying. I'm afraid of dying for no reason."

Winslow interjected. "Are you saying dyin' for our cause ain't no reason? There's two good men resting in an ice-covered grave that would argue otherwise." He was reaching a fever pitch.

MacIntosh didn't take his eyes off Grizz. "No, that's not my point. I'm saying let's live to fight another day. And let's fight a battle we can win."

"I've got a plan." Grizz took a step back and put his hand on Winslow's back. "Winslow's gonna pack up any of the finished product. We're gonna need it. Then we're gonna burn this place to the ground. The fire will hold them on the camp while we disappear."

"There'll be a fleet of cops waiting at the bottom of that road."

"Maybe. Maybe not. Doesn't matter. Road is impassable."

"If there's no way up here, then there's no way down," MacIntosh argued.

"There is, if you know your way around this neck of the woods. And I do. Know it better than just about anybody." Grizz bent his face close to Lawson's. "That means no need to keep this government whore alive any longer."

Lawson tried to meet his executioner's gaze with his one functional eye. Grizz dismissed his efforts with a snort and then rose back up to his full height.

"When Lank gets back, put a bullet in his head." Grizz cracked his knuckles. "Unless you'd like me to handle things for you?"

Lawson didn't hear MacIntosh's answer. The pulsing in his head intensified, continuing to resonate from its source, the empty hole where his right ear used to be. Lawson closed his eyes, fearing this time he would never open them again. He brought forward the memory of the fight he had with his wife before starting his day. Lawson paused it at the exact moment after the pickle jar shattered.

He looked deep into her hazel eyes. Beyond the anger and sadness, Lawson saw love. He held on to the freeze-framed image of his wife as he said his final goodbye.

He couldn't tell whether time had leapt forward or come to a screeching halt, but somewhere outside came a noise. Lawson heard a siren pierce the encroaching silence accompanying the slowing of his heartbeat. It became clearer, and his hopes faded as he realized it wasn't a siren at all.

It was a scream.

TWENTY-FOUR

HATCH PRESSED THE KIMBER CUSTOM II 45 CALIBER SEMI-AUTOMATIC handgun in front of her, letting it lead the way into the cafeteria. She held her breath as she stepped onto old boards that creaked as she walked. She kept a low profile, and kept her knees bent, maintaining a stable shooting platform.

Hatch was moving slower than normal but tried not to give credence to the torn ligaments in her ankle incessantly demanding attention with each step she took. The boot laces cinched tight would keep everything in place. She'd deal with the fallout later. There were more important tasks at hand.

She pushed the pain from her mind and focused her aim on the back half of the room. The cafeteria had been divided using bedsheets, tarps, and drop cloths strung across a clothesline. It was a poorly designed partition separating the clubhouse from the lab, and she marveled at the fact the idiots hadn't blown themselves up already.

The last thermal image that she had seen put Lawson on the other side of those sheets. And the fact that Grizz and the other members hovered around it like hornets protecting their queen gave Hatch good cause to believe he was still in there. She had hope he was still alive.

Hatch moved along the wall; her left shoulder close but not touching as she approached the gap in the partition. Without a moment's hesitation or a faltered step, Hatch pressed through the opening, letting the Kimber lead the way again. She brought the front sight up on the first target she saw. He stood in the center of the room, tying a rope to a backboard on the floor where Lawson was strapped.

MacIntosh turned. Hatch had her pistol up, pointed center mass, hovering over MacIntosh's heart. He had a small silver revolver in his right hand, which did not move. His trigger finger remained indexed alongside the frame.

Hatch scanned the room to make sure they were alone. "If you're the man I think you are, you're gonna need to trust me and drop that gun."

MacIntosh slowly shook his head. "I can't do that."

"Listen, if it's about going back, I've already talked to your parole officer. I can work it out."

"I'm not afraid of that."

"Then why aren't you dropping the gun?"

"Because there's something I've gotta do."

"There's no time for this." Hatch heard a banging and looked over her shoulder. "We've gotta go now."

"Where's Grizz?"

"I don't know, and that's why we have to go."

"Where's the rest of your team?"

Her gaze drifted to the floor. "It's just me."

"They sent one person?"

She shook her head. "No time to explain."

"Fine. I keep the gun, I come with you. If it'll make you feel better, I'll put it inside my waistband. I'll only draw it should the need arise."

MacIntosh did as he said. The pistol was now out of his hand, in the small of his back. Hatch got closer and saw that all of Deputy U.S. Marshal Calvin Lawson's wounds had been dressed, and better yet, he was alive. Though it looked like time was not on his side.

"That's your handiwork?"

"Yes ma'am. I've got him strapped to that board. Should hold. It's all I can do with what we've got."

"What are the straps for?"

"This." MacIntosh grabbed the straps and slowly hoisted Lawson up so that they were now back-to-back with the board in between them. "I've got him if you want to drive. I've got an ATV on the backside of the cafeteria. I was planning on making a run for it when you came in. Had to make this rig so I can get him out of here."

"You're here because of him?"

"No. My reason for being here is unrelated, but I'm not gonna let these savages kill an innocent man."

"Well, let's make sure he gets off this mountain alive." Hatch led the way.

MacIntosh was close behind. As Hatch came to the partition and prepared to step through, she heard the bang on the front door and spun to see the mismatched face of Frank Winslow. He was already firing when she turned.

She dove to the floor as four or five poorly placed shots peppered the lightweight partition. Hatch didn't hear the shattering of the meth lab vials. She didn't hear the explosion because in the moment that his last bullet passed by her head, she had fired three precision shots. Two in his chest and one dead center between his eyes. Winslow never fired another shot. He couldn't. He was dead before he hit the floor.

Hatch stood and turned to see MacIntosh with the revolver in his hand. He was facing her. She realized a split second too late why. A painter's drop cloth wrapped her up like a burrito as the enormous arms of The Way's leader plowed through from the burning kitchen. Hatch was pinned at the arms. The gun was now trapped beneath the thick canvas tarp, and she couldn't press it out enough to fire with any specificity as to where her round would land.

She threw back her head. The first blow connected with the top of the giant's forehead. He loosened his grip but didn't release her. In fact, he squeezed harder. Hatch struggled for air as she fought for her life. She continued to use the only weapon at her disposal. Her head. And she swung it like a blacksmith's hammer. This time, she connected with the bridge of his nose. Feeling his bone snap against the back of her head had the desired effect. His grip loosened enough that Hatch was able to then force her body free as she hit the ground, separating herself from the beast of a man.

She hadn't had time to clear the gun from the canvas still wrapped around it before he was back down on top of her. A massive fist the size of a boulder was rocketing toward her face when MacIntosh's first shot rang out. Two more followed. Grizz twisted violently to the right and then fell over onto his side.

Grizz was the recipient of two of the three rounds fired and had been thrown off course by the impact of the bullets. He twisted and fell backwards. He rolled once and then stopped. He was face down on a floor already stained and re-stained with Lawson's blood over the past twenty-four hours. Now Grizz's added to the mix.

Hatch freed her weapon and scrambled to her feet. There was no movement. The behemoth was down. If not permanently, at least for the moment.

Hatch closed in to verify. When she was two feet away, the kitchen exploded and sent a wall of fire across the room, singeing Hatch's hand and separating her from Grizz. The fire obliterated her view of the murderous gang leader.

Worse, it cut off her exit to the front door.

The fire had already jumped to the ceiling on the right side and was whipping its way around like a horse on a racetrack. The only exit was the side entrance she'd used earlier. MacIntosh waited with Lawson still strapped to his back as the fire closed in. He beckoned Hatch to hurry.

Hatch sprinted at full speed, taking each painful step with her damaged ankle in stride as the three of them burst through the now fully engulfed cafeteria door and onto the glacier outside.

Cool air fed the fire. Fingers of orange and red clawed at the departing trio as they ran to the awaiting ATV.

TWENTY-FIVE

HATCH'S SLOW SPEED HAD AS MUCH TO DO WITH CARGO AS IT DID THE terrain and weather. MacIntosh was back-to-back with her. He straddled the rear of the ATV to maintain control of Lawson and keep him as stable as possible while Hatch navigated the terrain. Although the ATV was equipped with all-weather tires, a fresh burst of snow added to the slickness and worked to blind her. The headlights of the ATV threw the snow's white glow only inches in front. Hatch tried to balance safety with survival, knowing Lawson's life was diminishing with each passing second.

"Where are we going?" MacIntosh called out over the howl of wind and roar of engine.

"You know where the ATV trail is?"

"Those are old mining trails."

"Whatever they are, that's how I plan on getting us out."

"Why can't we just shoot straight across?" MacIntosh said. "It drops off into a plateau, low land. You drop right off the glacier. It's faster."

"Not anymore. Unless you're Evel Knievel, this ATV isn't making it across. I heard them talking about the roads. It might not be much better."

"We'll cross that bridge when we get to it. First, we gotta make sure there's no more trolls under it. I know I hit Grizz."

"I know you did," she said. "But I like to confirm when a threat is neutralized. I don't like having things hanging over my head. Don't like looking over my shoulder."

"Neither do I. Didn't see him move after the fire and I didn't see him when we were out. If the bullets didn't kill him, I sure as hell hope the fire did."

The left tire caught a hard edge of ice that jerked the ATV. The backend fishtailed and Hatch fought to correct it.

"Is he okay?" she called back, not looking.

It was getting bumpier by the minute. Just as Hatch prepared to slow, the front two wheels of the ATV disappeared into an invisible hole. The blue-white and fresh snow made the glacier top glow, creating a visual washout, obscuring all potential hazards. One of them now gripped the front axle of the ATV, and before Hatch had time to even attempt to navigate them out, she was airborne.

Hatch wasn't able to see what happened to the ATV or anything else because a split second later, the top of her head slammed into the ground.

She landed on a steep decline and was sliding fast. The same ridges and jagged bumps that she had navigated with the ATV were now striking the exposed skin around her cheek and face. Hatch felt like she was skiing, snowplowing her way down a double diamond.

She extended her arms out in front of her, trying to slow her speed and mitigate the damage from the ice scraping and tearing at her skin. She then reached down with one hand, trying to activate the button to initiate the crampons, hoping to gain traction on the slippery slope and stop her rapid descent. The speed of the ATV when she had been tossed had only added to the speed at which she traveled now. She hoped to stop herself before she went into a deeper crevasse than the one that had sent them airborne.

Ice shaved off the ground and filled the inside lining of her jacket. The cold sting of the jagged pieces felt like a thousand hornets. She activated the left crampon and slammed down her foot. She was moving too fast to catch, and she moved faster by the second. All she could hear was wind and ice, and the scraping of her clothes and skin over the unforgiving landscape, until she came to a dead stop when a jagged shard of ice met her like a brick wall.

Her body twisted violently. Hatch was spinning now. A searing pain shot from her left shoulder. She worked to control her arm, but it banged loosely about. She was moving again until the side of her head collided with a rock.

Her eyelashes fought a losing battle to stop the relentless hurricane of sleet and snow that filled her view. The white then shifted to dark and she felt a warmth. She fought against it, but it was pulling hard.

She felt tired, and her eyes closed again. She fought to open them. As her vision started to fade and her eyes blurred, the last thing she saw was the shadow looming over her.

TWENTY-SIX

"HELP! ANYONE!" LANK CRIED OUT AGAIN FOR WHAT FELT LIKE THE million time, his throat raw.

He didn't even know if his words were penetrating the confines of his current prison. It was worse than any prison Lank had ever spent any time in. He'd trade the prefabricated faded green plastic of the Porta John he was trapped inside of for the cold, hard steel and concrete of a cell any day of the week. That woman had stabbed him in his injured foot. He hoped to return the favor someday, or worse.

Damn Winslow was a foot from that stupid door, and he didn't come and get me out.

Winslow tore off after the woman when he saw her slip in the side, and then there was Grizz. He barely made it off the porch. He wasn't sure if Grizz could see him in the Porta John, but he could feel his eyes through the cracks. He saw the disgust on his face. He knew he'd have to pay a price, and right now he couldn't imagine a worse one. After Winslow took off after the girl, the shooting started, and then the fire.

Lank had worked himself up onto the crapper's plastic seat and was in the process of getting his wrist restraints under his ankle when the cafeteria exploded. The force had knocked over the Porta John. It wobbled back and then fell to its side. Must've caught an edge because it flipped onto the door side, sealing it to the ice.

The concussive force of the exploding cafeteria had enough energy to slide the Porta John nearly thirty feet from where it had originally been located. Todd Lankowski was now lying face down on the door of the Porta John covered in urine and fecal matter donated by members of The Way.

Lank learned a valuable lesson that day. There isn't any amount of blue sanitizing liquid capable of masking the vile funk after being bathed in months' worth of human waste. Lank had given up any hope that anyone was coming to get him, and he was damn sure not going to die inside an outhouse on top of a burning glacier.

Lank began slamming upwards against the back end of the Porta John, using the force of his legs to try to crack the seams. He tried not to think about the filth he was pressing himself into as he bashed himself wildly around the inside until he felt a crack. After a brief but arduous struggle, Lank wormed himself through the plastic, bursting out like a Jack-in-the-Box.

He looked back to where the outhouse had been and the firelight of the still-burning cafeteria. A trail of blue and other horrible things marked its path to the final resting position where Lank now stood. He wanted to strip naked and clean himself from head to toe and burn his clothes in the cafeteria fire. He welcomed the wind because it worked to carry away some of the stink he'd collected.

The blue liquid coating his clothes had begun to freeze over. He started making his way toward the cabin for a change of clothes and to see if anyone else was alive. He looked back at the Porta John that had almost become his coffin. Grizz appeared on the other side of the porch, near where he and Winslow had parked their ATVs. He did not look pleased to see Lank.

"You good-for-nothing dipshit. I can't count on you for anything."

"I wasn't high, honest. It was that freaking MacIntosh and that crazy bitch. She caught me off guard. Look in my eyes, man."

Grizz did. He penetrated the depths of Lankowski's soul. "If I didn't know you and you weren't covered in shit and piss, I would take you by your neck and break it right here and leave you to die."

Grizz was bleeding from two gunshot wounds that Lank could see, one in the upper right shoulder and the second on the outside meat of his bicep on that same arm.

"You've been shot? Is it bad?"

Grizz took one step back and balled a fist. "Touch me with those shit-covered hands and it's the last thing you touch."

"Let me prove myself to you. I knew when we got up yesterday morning that it was gonna be my day, my day to prove that I was ready to follow, to be a true member of The Way, and to earn my Mark. Look, I screwed up. Let me make it right."

"None of them are leaving this mountain. Not today, not ever. You want to make things right with me? Let's start by finding them and making good on my promise." Grizz walked towards his ATV. "And I don't care if you have to ride around this mountain buck naked, you're not wearing those clothes anywhere near me. Hell, they'll be able to smell you six miles away."

Lank hobbled off to get a change of clothes from the bag he kept in one of the bunk rooms. He turned around and gave a big middle finger to the Porta John. His eyes followed the bloody trail that marked every time his right foot struck the icy ground. He thought about the man who'd shot him and the woman who'd stabbed him, and Lank planned on returning the favor tenfold.

He continued on the trail down to the cabin, and a few minutes later he was in dry clothes that no longer carried the horror of what he'd experienced.

"I heard them ride off." Lank said. "They had to have headed for the trails."

"They're gonna find a surprise when they get there. Sunrise is a couple hours away, and I don't want any one of them to ever see the light of it."

They started their ATVs and disappeared into the blizzard in the direction of the trails.

TWENTY-SEVEN

HATCH WOKE TO THE SMELL OF FIRE. SHE BLINKED AWAY THE COBWEBS and managed to open her left eye halfway. The flicker of firelight entered her vision.

She tried to sit up, but her left arm was tied tight around her waist. She reached for her Kimber with her right. Her holster was empty. She tried to sit up again.

"Easy. You took a bad spill." It was MacIntosh's voice.

"My gun?"

"Looked for it. Didn't see it. You came down that ice about the length of three football fields and you were moving fast. Picked up what I could. Which wasn't much."

"My eye." She brought her free hand up and felt the softball-size lump on the right side of her face.

He moved forward and crouched as if he were performing an examination. "Took a pretty good beating on that ice. Most of it is superficial ice burn, but the stuff around your right eye, it's cut pretty good. I'm not sure if it got your cornea or not. I put some antibacterial ointment on the wounds. Cleaned them as best I could with what I had."

"What about Lawson?" Hatch looked around the makeshift camp.

MacIntosh retreated to his previous position. "He's doing okay."

Hatch followed MacIntosh's gaze over to Lawson on the other side of the fire, where he was now strapped into a cot. The dressings on his wounds had been refreshed. The man appeared to be sound asleep. His chest rose and fell gently.

"Where are we?" Hatch had trouble bringing up her internal map of the area.

"Old mineshaft. Here, let me help you up." MacIntosh reached over and assisted Hatch. Her left shoulder was sore. "I popped it back in when you were out, but that thing was badly dislocated. I'm pretty sure you tore something."

"Good splint." She admired his handiwork.

"Thanks."

As she sat up, the room spun, and she almost fell back to the cot.

MacIntosh steadied her. "That wound is gonna need some stitches. I packed it good, but you really did some damage when you hit that rock like a freight train."

"Noted." Hatch reeled from nausea. She shook it off. "We gotta get him on the move. How long have I been out?"

"Two hours."

"Two hours?"

"I was able to run an IV drip, get some fluids back into him. I have a full med bag. Though, between the two of you, I'm running out of supplies fast."

Hatch now noticed that he had rigged up an IV drip next to the cot. He had basically converted the mineshaft into a triage medical tent, and he'd done well by both his patients.

She pulled out her cell phone.

MacIntosh shook his head. "Good luck getting signal up here."

"Punching the message in so as soon as we get it, I can hit send." She took a couple of unsteady steps before regaining her footing. The empty feeling in the pit of her stomach vanished, replaced with a steel resolve. "Let's get him situated on the ATV and get the hell out of here."

"Not gonna be that easy. ATV is trashed. That thing's in about seventeen different parts on the same hill you went for a slide on."

"Then what other options do we have?"

"The only way we're getting out of here is on foot."

"How far are we from the main road from here?"

"A mile."

Hatch looked at the unconscious marshal laying on the cot and then down at her splinted arm. "We're gonna have to make it work."

"Just take a second and rest. Let me get him rigged up. I'll tether him like a sled and pull him. It'll be no problem."

Hatch let MacIntosh set about his business as she warmed herself by the fire. She looked at him as he knotted a rope to the ends of the cot and created a pulley system. He checked his knots. He was thorough.

"Why'd you do all this?" Hatch asked.

MacIntosh dismissed her with a wave. "Does it matter?"

"I read your file."

"Didn't matter to cops. Didn't matter to the judge when I told him what they had done to my girlfriend. They still locked me up. The system's broken, and then it keeps breaking other people. That's the way it works unless you choose not to let it. I was put into the foster care system early.

"I didn't know my father, and my mom sold me for drugs, but one thing came out of it. My brother, he was the only thing that kept me going. When I was twelve, I ended up in a foster family, and they had brought me in along with another foster. We were about the same age and, well, at first, we hated each other and fought all the time. We took every bad home experience out on the parents trying to give us a better life and we took it out on each other too. But our parents cared. They never quit on us. And over time, we became a family. The fights we had were fights all brothers have, and over the two years I lived with them, I had my first official taste of family."

"Why only two years?"

"Car accident killed them both."

"I'm so sorry."

"Wasn't your fault. But what are you gonna do at fourteen? We weren't biological brothers, so like I said, a broken system breaks people. They broke up the one bit of family I had a chance of holding onto and sent us into different foster camps. We kept in touch though we traveled different paths. I saw an opportunity in the Marine Corps, and he got himself mixed up in drugs. But I never stopped caring about him. Planned to help him out. Half the reason I became a medic was because I wanted to learn how to help people, and he was gonna be my first real patient, the first person I really saved."

Hatch wanted to connect the dots. "How'd you end up on that assault case?"

"After I got out of the Corps, I was working as a paramedic and doing all right. I had a family, a girlfriend with a kid on the way. I was off duty and coming home from work when I happened upon a drive-by shooting. Saw some guy gunned down in the middle of the street." MacIntosh shook his head. "I was the first one there. I jumped out and did what I did. I always keep a med bag with me. Old habits, I guess. Plugged enough holes and he survived."

"I don't understand how that led to your arrest."

"That's the thing. I guess doing a good deed doesn't always have a reward because it turned out the guy I saved was some big-time gang leader, and the people who shot him were big-time in their gang too."

It came together for Hatch. "You ruined their hit."

"Might've slipped under the radar had the media not gotten wind of it and made a big show of it. They put my name in the newspaper. Put my picture on the front page. Called me a hero. I was at work when they came for me."

The room grew quiet. Even the fire seemed to have stopped to listen.

MacIntosh's face grew dark. "I wasn't home, but my girl was." His gaze shifted away. "They hurt her. When the court failed to prosecute, I hurt them."

"But you didn't kill them."

"No, I didn't. I wish I had, though. Maybe I wouldn't have gotten caught."

"Fast forward for me," Hatch said. "You were three weeks from getting out on those assault charges. What changed?"

MacIntosh chuckled, though his face looked anything but happy. "Everything. I got news that my brother had been killed. I call him that, you know. People have told me I'm crazy, but he's the only family I've got. Had..." He took a moment to compose himself. "I had planned to come out and kill Grizz. You're right, I was three weeks out. You make a lot of enemies in prison, especially when you don't join up."

"Join up?"

"Pick sides. Join a gang. Anyway, at Spring Creek, there were two big rival Aryan gangs. I had pissed one of them off when I wouldn't do what they asked me to."

"What did they ask you to do?"

"He wanted what everybody wants inside there, a favor, a trade. But see, some of these guys that you say no to, they hold a grudge, and I didn't join up with anybody. My plan was to get in, do my time, and get out. Had been pretty good at it, but three weeks out, they came for me, and I killed them."

Hatch noted the sorrow on his face. She opened her mouth to speak, but had nothing to offer.

"I'm not proud of it. I tried to avoid it."

"Sometimes killing is unavoidable."

MacIntosh nodded. "Sometimes it is. When I killed that guy, I gained the attention of Red Winslow. I knew his affiliation with The Way. I figured, hell, I had some time to burn. I might as well get as close as possible, making sure that when I got out of there, killing Grizz would be the first stop I made. It would be a lot better if he welcomed me into his home so I could look him in the eye before taking his life."

"You know, you don't have to do this."

He snorted. "Give me a break."

"You can disappear. Help me get down to where the ATV trail meets the road. I've got a vehicle there. It'll get you into town and you can disappear. I'll tell parole–"

"No," MacIntosh interrupted. "I don't run from my problems. I face them square on. I run now, then I'm running the rest of my life."

Hatch thought about this and the year she'd spent on the run, only to be working with people who tried to take her life. "Then, let's finish this thing." Hatch stood. Her legs wobbled only a moment before she steadied and readied herself for the mile trek down the glacier.

"You're gonna love Jessie," Hatch said.

"Who's Jessie?"

"Our ticket off this popsicle."

TWENTY-EIGHT

THE CLOUDS DISSIPATED, GIVING WAY TO A HALF MOON SITTING HIGH IN the sky. It illuminated their path as they headed down the last stretch of glacier before reaching the place where it transitioned into the muddy ATV trail. Hatch saw the porcupine looking E350. She scanned the area, looking for any potential threat. No sign of the ATVs. No sign of Grizz or Lankowski.

"I hope you're as good at changing a tire as you are at fixing the wounded," Hatch said.

"I'm no AAA, but I'm sure I can manage." MacIntosh cracked a smile. Amid the rough exterior, there was a kindness in his eyes, brightened by his smile.

"I wish the owner was here to greet you but meet Jessie." Hatch extended her one good arm in the direction of the satellite antenna-covered quake tracker/painter's truck.

"She looks like a Jessie," MacIntosh said. "If I can get this tire up and we can get it out of the mud, we can use the van to get him out of here."

"That was my plan. Hell of a lot better than walking."

Hatch walked to the back end of the van. She opened the back doors and MacIntosh brought Lawson in his sled gurney.

"Let's get him out of the cold." MacIntosh moved to one side.

"Good idea." Hatch squatted and assisted, guiding it with her good hand. MacIntosh did the brunt of the work. After they had Lawson loaded, he said, "All right, let's see about getting that spare."

Hatch looked down at the ice and saw blood. For a second, she thought it belonged to Lawson, but MacIntosh had bandaged his wounds. The bleeding hadn't stopped, but they weren't dripping. She lifted her gaze, relaxing her eyes so they unfocused and took in all movement. Hatch saw the glimmer of steel.

"Ambush!" Hatch shoved MacIntosh to the ground just before the first shots fired, loud bangs followed by the plink of metal as the rounds struck Jessie's steel side.

Hatch began low crawling, pulling herself along the ice and mud, toward the front end of the vehicle. The shots stopped for a moment.

"I spotted Lankowski," she said. "Any sign of Grizz?"

"Maybe I got him back at the camp? Maybe the fire did?" MacIntosh moved to the rear of the vehicle, catching up to Hatch.

Lankowski remained hidden behind a well-fortified position of rock and tree. His cackling filled the silent void like a circus clown gone mad.

"You've got one bullet in the gun. Make it count." MacIntosh tossed the revolver to Hatch. In his haste, he overshot both Hatch and the cover of the van. The five-shot revolver now lay several feet away in the snow-covered mud in front of the van's front end. "Shit!"

Hatch worked herself toward the front of the vehicle. Gunfire continued, but more sporadically, less focused with both men out of sight. And then it stopped altogether. Hatch had made her way to the front right wheel well and was peering under when she saw Lankowski with a gun in hand, peeking out from behind a set of trees not ten feet away. He'd been on the move in between his bursts of fire.

Rounds continued to pelt the left side of Hill's beloved Jessie. The side panel took most of the abuse. Two bullets struck both left side tires, flattening them and reducing Hatch's ability to peer out from underneath.

"I'll draw his fire." MacIntosh shook his legs out like a sprinter reading himself at the blocks.

No time to argue. They need the gun. One bullet was better than none. "On my mark."

"You just make sure you get to that gun." He offered a weak smile.

Hatch pulled herself through the cold mud as she edged to the front right tire, and the edge of her cover. She looked over at MacIntosh and gave a thumbs up.

MacIntosh launched forward and was immediately stopped short by a large forearm. Grizz hooked his arm around MacIntosh's throat and pulled him to the rear of the van. Lankowski took more time between his shots, focusing his aim on Hatch's position.

MacIntosh was at least six-two, and if Hatch had to guess between two-hundred-twenty and two-hundred-forty pounds, most of which was muscle hardened over six years in the penitentiary. Even with those stats he was nothing more than a rag doll in the arms of Walter Grizzly.

His nose broken, this time Grizz was wiser to the attack. Grizz pinned MacIntosh's other arm behind him and was choking the life out of him. Even with two bullet holes in his arm, he was able to maintain a grip that MacIntosh couldn't break.

Lankowski began firing again. Hatch couldn't get to the gun and instead took cover, using the wheel well and engine block as a shield. She saw MacIntosh escape Grizz's clutch. He sprinted away but only managed twenty feet of separation before tripping on an obstacle. And then came a roar from the side, like a charging bear. Grizz slammed his body into MacIntosh like a rhinoceros on full charge.

Hatch turned to see Grizz mauling MacIntosh, slamming his huge arms against MacIntosh's face and body like a gorilla defending his pride. MacIntosh deflected the blows as best he could. He met force with force, kicking and punching where opportunity provided. In the end, the behemoth was able to control him.

Grizzly performed a move Hatch had only seen in a pro wrestling match. The red bearded leader of The Way reached down and snatched MacIntosh by the throat. In a feat of strength, he raised him off the ground, above the height of Jessie's roof.

Hatch could see the life draining from MacIntosh's eyes. He fought valiantly, even digging a thumb into one of the bullet holes, which only seemed to anger Grizz further, who then started slamming MacIntosh's skull into the Ford's backend. Blood seeped from the side of his head in multiple places.

Hatch needed to level the playing field, peering around the front end of the tire just under where the muddy ground met the thick rubber wall, now deflated and torn. The reason they had not made it. The reason Jessie had been left.

She was looking for an opportunity to make a dive for the gun when the front end of the van lurched forward. Lankowski's head dipped out of view. The van was now rocking back and forth as Grizzly rammed MacIntosh's face into the rear door. Hatch unzipped her right boot, pressed the button to extend the crampon, and flung the boot to MacIntosh.

"Heads up!"

He caught the boot in midair and swung it over his head, slashing Grizzly's face. Bright red blood coated Grizz from the top of his head down to his beard. MacIntosh slammed a fist into the soft spot on Grizz's throat with enough force to free the chokehold. MacIntosh fell to the ground next to the spiked crampon.

Grizz launched on top of him again, preparing to deliver another savage beating, one that MacIntosh would unlikely survive. He raised his arm to deliver a blow, and in that moment of opportunity, MacIntosh struck out with the crampon, slamming it into the side of Grizz's throat, giving it a hard tug to the right and then left.

The fist in midair was never delivered. Grizz stepped back. Blood the color of his beard poured out from the side of his neck, and for the first time, Hatch saw fear in the big man's eyes as he staggered back gurgling.

With Lankowski momentarily distracted by Grizz's situation, Hatch capitalized on it and launched herself the six feet to the gun. Rolling and sliding across the mud, she came up and tried to find Grizz in his sights.

Grizz roared and disappeared behind the back of the van before Hatch could get a shot off. Hatch turned her attention back to Lankowski, but he was gone, no longer popping his head out or firing rounds. A second later, he appeared, stepping out from cover, but not by his own volition. He was now gripped in the same way MacIntosh had been, although this time Grizz only used one arm to restrain the much thinner and weaker man as he held him aloft.

That didn't stop Lankowski from cursing and kicking wildly at the legs of the big man, all the while begging to be released and questioning why. The answer was simple. Grizz was afraid. He was a coward. The big man was using the smaller man to hide behind, and he was doing a good job of using the thin meth addict's body to shield his vitals. With only one shot, Hatch had to make it count.

Lankowski still had a gun and she had to assume Grizz had one too, although he seemed to take great pleasure in using his hands for his dirty work.

He made a mistake in picking Lankowski as his shield. The gaunt meth addict flailed. In a moment of desperation, he bit into the thick forearm of his leader, enough so that he broke the skin, but not with enough force that he was able to break free. It was just enough pain to force a grunt from Grizz. In that slight movement, a target presented. His head.

As he stepped back and neared the gaping hole that had formed during the big quake, Hatch fired the revolver's last shot.

The shot struck Grizz as he shifted and impacted the right side of his head cutting a bloody path starting from the corner of his eyebrow and disappearing to the back of his head. He staggered back, and now he was less than a foot from the edge of the gaping hole that had formed during the big quake.

Hatch stood up and faced off with the behemoth who was less than fifteen feet away. Hatch lowered her center of gravity, digging her right bootless right into the cold muddy earth, and prepared to charge. Before she could take a step, the ground shook. Hatch was knocked over by the tremors.

When Hatch looked up again, Lank and Grizz along with the strip of land they were standing on, were gone.

TWENTY-NINE

"Help!" Lankowski squealed. His shrieking intensified.

Hatch leaned over the edge. Looking down, she saw an unexpected sight. Lankowski's jacket was twisted and hooked along a jagged bit of root, effectively latching him to the wall of the crevasse. Gripping tightly to his leather belt was the giant Grizz. The oversized belt buckle seemed to be holding it all together. Lankowski was desperately holding onto the branch.

"I'm going to rip your arms off and feed 'em to you when I get out of this!" Grizz told his counterpart.

Hatch stood with her hands on her hips and looked down at giant, literally hanging by a thread. "I don't think you're getting out."

He growled. It was almost comical, the huge man hanging off Lankowski's toothpick-like frame. Grizz's weight was pulling them both down as he tried to climb up.

"You're gonna pull me off the branch! Stop!" Lankowski yelled. Grizz didn't stop. Lankowski did something she didn't expect to see. He pulled a folding knife from his back pocket.

"What are you doing?" Grizz boomed.

"I know I told you I'd follow you anywhere. But this ain't happening! I'm not dying for you!"

Grizz's eyes flashed with anger. He made a desperate attempt to pull his girth up, as he clung to Lankowski's leather belt. The man who'd just been used as a human shield was now being used as a ladder.

Lankowski sawed his leather belt. It was a race for survival, and there could be only one winner.

In the instant the knife severed the final bit of leather, Grizz's eyes went from unadulterated hatred to pure fear as he fell backwards into the dark, deep crevasse, still holding onto the belt.

Hatch never heard him hit the ground. She kept her focus on the remaining man. "Drop the knife."

Lankowski snarled "Help me up." He was stuck ten feet below the ground where Hatch and MacIntosh stood.

"I think you're good right there," Hatch said.

"What? You're just gonna leave me here?"

"That's the idea," Hatch said. "It'll give you time to reflect about your *Way* of life."

"You can't just leave me here!"

"Don't worry, I know somebody who's really good about getting people out of situations like yours." Hatch thought of Babiarz.

Lankowski released his right arm from its death grip. Using his knife like an ice axe, he shoved it into the side of the crag to anchor himself and tried to pull himself up.

Lankowski's clothes were still twisted in the tree root. Wriggling wildly and cursing profusely, he continued his endless stream of murderous threats he intended to make good on should he got topside. He seemed to grow less fearful and more angry by the second. He tore at his clothes. The right pocket of his jacket was the only thing still holding him back.

Hatch readied herself to subdue him should he make the climb out. But one hard jerk of his jacket removed any need. Lankowski freed himself from the tree, but in the process he also freed the only thing keeping him anchored. His knife.

Lankowski's shrill cry reverberated off the dirt walls as he disappeared into darkness. Wind drowned out the whine of Lankowski's last words.

Hatch turned to MacIntosh. "You know, you can run now. Disappear. I can tell them whatever you need. I can tell them, that you died saving me. This can be a fresh start for you. Last chance to reconsider."

MacIntosh looked at her. "I don't think so."

She felt the question on her face.

"It's not who I am," he said. "I face everything head-on and if I run now, I'll be running the rest of my life. I prefer to take whatever's coming to me. Good, bad, or somewhere in between, whatever I have coming to me, I've earned. And I'll take the licks knowing that I did the right thing, even if I went about it in the wrong way."

Hatch surveyed their options of getting across the recently opened trench in the direction of their final destination and help. Only one thing came to mind. "How are you with heights?"

THIRTY

HATCH AND MACINTOSH REMOVED THE THIRTY-TWO-FOOT ALUMINUM collapsible Werner ladder. Hatch scanned the gap, looking for the closest point to them that would get them over to the landing zone.

"I'm gonna need you to go first," Hatch said to MacIntosh.

He exhaled slowly. "If I'm gonna be honest, crossing a bottomless pit on a rickety ladder in high winds is not on my bucket list."

"That makes two of us."

They located a spot on the edge of the divide where it narrowed to a gap of about twenty feet across. They extended the ladder the entire thirty-two feet, each of them holding one side to balance it against the wind. Hatch was grateful that the wind had subsided partially since last night.

Working in concert, they controlled the rate of the ladder's descent as they levered it across the chasm. They dropped it the last several feet. It clanged and bounced once. MacIntosh stepped on one of the rungs to stop it from moving.

"I'll hold it while you two cross," Hatch insisted.

"Why don't you go with him?" MacIntosh asked.

"Because you got him here. If it wasn't for you, he'd already be dead. Take him across the finish. I'll be on this end to hold it. Just make sure you're on the other side to return the favor when it's my turn."

MacIntosh apparently wasn't joking about the heights thing. Neither was Hatch. But just as her father had taught her those many years ago in the back mountains behind their house, fear is to be accepted. Fear is to be cherished. The greatest warriors recognize it in themselves, and therefore are able to recognize it in others and capitalize on it. The bravest people Hatch had ever met faced fear on a regular basis, something MacIntosh was demonstrating as he edged himself over the dark void.

He had worked the strap around his waist, giving him the easiest balance. He kept the rope at his center point as he shimmied his way on all fours, crawling ahead and dragging the unconscious Lawson behind him on the makeshift sled gurney across the gap.

Hatch guided the bottom of the gurney reaching out as far as she could while maintaining her weight on her end of the ladder to hold it in place. MacIntosh and Lawson were on their own now, moving across the middle.

A nasty gust of wind kicked up, throwing more dusty snow into the bright sky, casting glitter all around and causing it to slide. It edged to the right and Hatch fought to contain it on her end, but the combined weight of the two men along the span made it very tough. MacIntosh was only a few feet from getting himself across the newly formed gorge when the back end of Lawson's gurney fishtailed off the edge of the gurney.

Before the weight could teeter enough to drag MacIntosh and Lawson to their death, the former Marine and ex-con dove off the end of the ladder, pulling Lawson with him. He skidded to a stop on the other side. MacIntosh held a shaky thumbs up, accompanied by a forced smile.

"Easy as pie," he called across.

"I don't know what kind of pie you eat." She saw it got a laugh. Hatch allowed herself one too. Laughter was always good for shaking off the nerves.

She got down on all fours just as MacIntosh had and began quickly crawling across, not wasting any time. There was a small lull in the wind, and she wanted to capitalize on it. MacIntosh held firm. She could see the tension in the grip, his knuckles white. He put all his weight down, holding the ladder in place.

Hatch was nearly to the other side when the wind picked up again. But it wasn't the wind that sent a shiver down her spine. It was the low rumble she heard just behind it.

THIRTY-ONE

HATCH WAS RELIEVED TO SEE THE RUMBLE WAS CREATED BY THE ROTORS of the returning FBI Black Hawk, this time accompanying a medical chopper. After Hatch reached the other side of the gorge, she took up one end of the rope tied to Lawson, and MacIntosh took the other. The two shouldered the burden of Lawson's weight equally as they hustled the last quarter mile across flatter ground to the landing zone.

Hatch put the great divide and Camp Hope behind her as the helicopters landed, driving away the fresh snow from last night, throwing it into the air as the sunrise broke through the last bit of gray. It now danced in the light and gave an angelic shimmer to the responding medical and law enforcement rescue team.

Hatch was pleased to see Agent Babiarz and her partner Agent Medina. Just as they'd done when she brought in Cruise, they hustled to her and met at the halfway point, taking the burden and allowing Hatch and MacIntosh to slow their walk, which enabled Hatch to favor her stronger leg over her injured ankle.

"Nice job on these bandages," one of the medics said to Hatch.

She shook her head and threw a thumb to MacIntosh who was standing beside her. "Credit for all this..." She pointed to her sling and bandaged head, then at Lawson. "...and all that there goes to this man."

"That's why it pains me to do this." Cal Roe, commander of the FBI's Hostage Rescue Team stepped into view.

"I've got to put you in cuffs," he said to MacIntosh.

Hatch stepped in between the two men. Roe widened his stance. His facial expression implied he did not like the challenge Hatch presented. The glance he cast to the side, also told Hatch that he especially did not like the challenge in front of two of his operators.

"I don't get on that helicopter if he goes in cuffs. If MacIntosh hadn't been there, Lawson and I wouldn't be coming down from this mountain outside of a body bag."

"You're not in a position to make demands. Listen, what you did back there was nothing short of amazing. And the fact that you're willing to stand and vouch for this man speaks volumes to that. I know there's more to this guy, but right now, he's on a parole remand and I have to see that through." He then directed his comments to MacIntosh. "These cuffs can come off as easy as they go on."

MacIntosh nodded and extended his wrists. "I'll take whatever's coming my way.

Roe's hand hovered with his cuffs. "If what she said is true, we'll do our best to figure some things out for you on the backend of this."

Roe placed MacIntosh into custody and escorted him aboard the bird. Medina and Babz were assigned to look over Lawson and were riding in the medical chopper with him. Just before Hatch climbed aboard the FBI helicopter, she called over to the female HRT operator.

"Agent Babiarz?"

The female operator turned and took a step closer and smiled. "Babz."

"Babz, I just wanted to tell you, that was a hell of a thing I saw you do yesterday."

Babz waved her off. "It was nothing."

"Don't be modest. I know a lot of brave people who wouldn't have done what you did, and several people are alive right now *because* you did it."

Hatch turned to head back to her helicopter.

"Any advice for the new kid on the block?" Babz called out as Hatch climbed aboard.

"When the opportunity presents, never miss."

"I never do."

The rotors whipped up to speed and less than a minute later, Hatch was airborne, and Lawson's life now rested with the medical team working to save it.

As the helicopter went up, Hatch looked down on the glacier. The cracks in the ice seemed smaller. The glacier itself seemed less menacing in the light of day. Their flight out took them over Camp Hope, and the black scar burned into the glacier where the cafeteria used to be.

THIRTY-TWO

MONITORS BEEPED, AND FANS WHIRRED IN THE BACKGROUND. HATCH sat beside the man on the bed, her scarred right arm resting on the mattress, their skin touching. Her left arm was still in a sling. Cruise was preparing for a second surgery that was designed to stabilize him before traveling back to California. He had been in Alaska's Regional Hospital in Anchorage for the past two days.

Cruise looked up at Hatch. The light above shrunk his pupils, bringing out the cobalt and tiny flecks of gold lining the edge of his irises.

She had gotten lost in those eyes before, and since being back in the man's presence, she found herself fighting the urge to do so again. His hand slid across the top of hers. He rolled a gentle finger back and forth, brushing the scar that lined the edge of her wrist. She didn't retract this time, embracing the warmth of his hand.

Cruise had been given a heavy sedative and it was beginning to work its magic, as evidenced by his droopy eyelids and slow speech. "I can say without even speaking to Tracy, the Talon job is yours if you want it. I don't think anyone's ever shown practical skills like the ones you've displayed recently. And I sure as hell never thought boots could be used as a weapon," he said.

"Try walking a mile in my shoes," Hatch replied.

"I don't know if I want to after what you did walking a mile in mine." He laughed at his own joke. "Look at us. Who would've thought?

"Let's not do this. Not now."

"No better time than the present. In my world, you know what they say about the only easy day being yesterday. But I like to look forward to some easy days ahead with you."

"Let's talk about this some other time."

"It could've worked, you know. Us. No one gets you better than me, and vice versa. It'll take me a while to get back up on my feet anyway. It could be a good time to see if there's still something there."

The last few words dripped out slowly, like the IV taped into his wrist. Hatch started to reply, but he cut her off.

"Talon will be there if you want it, and it will be a distant memory if you don't. You know, you can go back now, free and clear. But what does that give you? I think you know the life that's waiting for you back there, and maybe if you looked deep inside yourself, I don't think that life will ever be for you."

Hatch thought on those words. Cruise knew her well. He was part of her old world, the one that made sense. Also, the one that had turned its back on her. It presented opportunity again.

She patted the top of his hand just below where the IV was taped. "Let's talk about this later."

"There's the Hatch I know. You getting ready to pop smoke and disappear?"

"I just said we'll talk later."

"I know you. You won't be here when I wake up. I can see it in your eyes. You want to run. I don't know if it's me or Talon you're running from, or maybe there's something you're running to. Perhaps someone? I dunno, Hatch. We haven't had a chance to catch up." He pushed his cheeks up into a weak smile and tried to wink.

"We had our run, and that was years ago. It was good. Hell, it was great, but it's over. Life moves on. Things are different. Complications that weren't there then are present now. You and I have grown a lot in the time since we've been apart. Who even knows if we would like each other anymore?"

"That's what I'm saying. Stick around long enough for us to find out."

Hatch wanted to push away. He was stripping down her walls. She didn't like it. She felt exposed. She felt guilty. She thought of Savage. Yet, her eyes remained locked on Cruise, and she knew the power he held over her.

He continued. "And it wasn't that we didn't work out before. The military tore us apart. We were in two different services thrown into different directions even though we were from the same world."

"Then what would be different this time?"

"We'd be on the same team if you choose. Or hell, maybe it's time for me to step back." He weakly tapped at the leg going in for its second surgery. "I'm no spring chicken. I'm not asking you to marry me. I'm asking you to come back to California with me. I'm asking you to be here when I wake up."

Hatch opened her mouth to speak, but no words came out. Cruise was a good man and he needed help getting back on his feet. Hatch had already punished those responsible for this tragedy, and so for once, she decided to do something that she'd never done before. Hatch decided to stop punishing herself.

She'd looked death in the face so many times and had grown so comfortable with the thought of her own demise that it had overshadowed any chance of her own happiness. She looked down at Cruise, his eyelids at half mast, the blue tucked into a medical slumber, and she had a question that she didn't know the answer to. Could Cruise be her chance at happiness?

Facing this fear was scarier than crossing the divide. This fear exposed what Hatch protected most above all else...her heart. She leaned forward, bringing her lips close to his right ear. Her breath tickled his flesh as she whispered the words, "I promise." Then sealed it with a kiss on his forehead just before his eyes closed completely.

Hatch sat back, and then to her surprise caught a glimpse of Commander Jordan Tracy balancing himself on a crutch and brace in the doorway. He held his hands up in defense and had a cheeky smile.

"No need to explain. This is off company hours, of course. But obviously, if you want to come work for us at Talon, any personal relationship you have must remain outside of work."

"That will never be an issue." Hatch felt embarrassed for even having to defend it. "About working with Talon, I'm gonna be honest, I'm still up in the air."

Tracy shrugged. "Well, I brought you in to show you the bells and whistles of how we run an op, and instead I showed you a complete and utter shit show. I do hope to have your decision sooner rather than later. With the team in its current state, I will be looking to add resources where I can."

"No need to apologize for how the op played out. If it had gone smoothly, maybe I wouldn't have seen the things that really mattered."

"Like what?"

"If a unit's not truly tested, how will they ever prove they can rise in the face of adversity? I got to see Talon when you were knocked down on your ass. I got to see a commander willing to break some rules and make calls that others would've been afraid to make, and those decisions saved lives. I saw the way the team worked together when it mattered, and I saw the way they cared about each other when it went sideways. As far as my impression of Talon, it's definitely changed. But let's just leave it at that for now. I'm gonna stick around for a little bit. I made a promise."

He started to retreat and stopped. "Hey, I was able to get that address you asked for. Here it is."

It was scribbled on a torn sheet of paper. Hatch looked at the address, and then folded it and put it in her pocket.

"After you take care of that business, head back to the hangar," Tracy said. "A car will be waiting for you. Once Cruise and Hertzog are stabilized, we're gonna transport them back to California."

"Any word on Lawson?"

"I just spoke to the doctor. He's critical, but they were able to stabilize his worst wounds. He's gonna make it."

"All thanks to MacIntosh. Speaking of MacIntosh, I know that the HRT commander had mentioned looking into his criminal history and getting some things straightened out. I was wondering, with

Talon's skill at erasing and rewriting history, maybe you could give him a chance at having a truly fresh start?"

"I don't think I've ever met anyone more deserving," Tracy's eyes were serious. "Aside from you. And for what it's worth, seeing what you did up there on that glacier, and knowing your father the way I did, you honor him with your life and everything you've done with it. I hope you know that."

"Thank you, sir." Hatch extended a hand to the Talon commander, and then gave one last look to Cruise, his eyes still closed, the cobalt sealed until the medication released its hold.

Hatch headed to the hallway and down towards the elevators. She pulled the address from her pocket and punched it into her GPS.

The elevator opened a moment later and she headed out for one more stop before leaving Alaska behind.

THIRTY-THREE

Hatch drove the Land Rover Talon had lent her. It was much like the other two, one swallowed by the river, the other swallowed by the land.

Hatch thought of Taylor and finding his twisted body, the image still fresh by its recentness. The Taylor situation made her think of that day in Afghanistan. The one that forever changed her life, the lives of everyone there, and the lives of those who weren't, like the wife and daughter who awaited a father's homecoming that never came.

Hatch knew the scar of that day was far deeper and far more twisted; an old wound that needed closing, and she planned to do it when she got back. *Can't move forward if you're stuck in the past,* her father had said. It was her father's memory that kept her trapped for twenty years. She had avenged his wrongful death and released its burden, but quickly found after there were still many demons left.

She tuned out the noise in her head by turning up the volume on the radio. She found a news station that had just come back from commercial break and was updating the audience on what had transpired the day before. Hatch let the over-exaggerated ramblings of the radioman's delivery dampen her mind's wanderings.

"Incredible news out of Breakneck, Alaska. Not less than two days ago, a shooting that left one Marshal dead and the other wounded and kidnapped ended in a blaze of fire. Reports are coming in that while in captivity, the series of earthquakes that shook the ground over the twenty-four-hour period had somehow..." The broadcast cut to static before returning. "It appears the cafeteria at Camp Hope had been turned into a crystal meth laboratory.

"And during the tumultuous ground activity, a fire broke out and eventually caused the entire cafeteria to explode. Miraculously though, Deputy U.S. Marshal Calvin Lawson survived. Although having been shot the day before and beaten and mutilated during his captivity, the deputy will recover.

"In an even stranger turn of events, law enforcement said that a couple hikers who happened to be in the area came across the fire and found Lawson. A male and female managed to get him across a crevasse and over to the safety of the FBI. If that wasn't enough for you folks, you've got to tune into the TV and see a rescue that took place during one of the attempts to recover the kidnapped Lawson.

"I'm watching it again right now. You wouldn't believe what I'm saying if you haven't seen it already. A female FBI agent, Laura Babiarz, climbed down into a helicopter where the ground split, hanging on by the grace of God. And guess what she did, folks? She brought the commander out. Carried him out on her back. I've watched this thing a hundred times. But people like this FBI agent and whoever those two anonymous hikers were, gives this old reporter hope."

Hatch turned the radio off, followed the GPS location to the pin up ahead on the right. She parked the Land Rover in front of a two-story colonial with a detached garage. She wasn't looking for the homeowner. Hatch walked around the side of the house to where a ladder extended to the second-floor window. She looked up at the man at the top, using a wide flat metal scraper to remove the old paint from the wood lathing.

"She's a pretty good ladder." Hatch's voice startled the man.

Burton Hill came down the ladder like a kid on Christmas morning. "I didn't think I was gonna get to see you again."

"I'm trying to do a better job of making my peace before I depart," Hatch said.

"Pretty good rule of thumb," Hill responded.

"I just wanted to stop by and thank you for what you did at the river and on the mountain."

"I'd do it again in a heartbeat if you'd ask."

"I know you would. That friend of mine you helped me save, he wanted to thank you too."

Hatch watched as Burton Hill's chest swelled up with pride.

"I wanted to give you something. Something I've held onto for too long."

Hill cocked an eyebrow as Hatch reached inside her front pocket to fish it out. She opened her palm and handed it to him.

As he held up the circular patch in front of his face, Hatch said, "I figured maybe you could find room for one more."

"What is it? I've never seen this unit before. Is that an eagle?"

"No, it's a banshee. You haven't seen it because it never existed."

His thumb ran across the burn mark, across its center. Then he looked at her arm and he nodded without speaking. Both let the silence hang in the air for a moment before Hill broke it.

"Where to next?"

"The corner of everywhere and nowhere."

Hill laughed and didn't ask for any explanation. She reached out a hand and Hill instead rose to a salute in perfect form. Hatch snapped her heels together, locked her body into the position of attention, and delivered Aerographer's Mate Third Class Burton Hill his proper return.

Hatch then turned and walked back towards the Land Rover. "You take care of yourself. The world needs good men like you."

"It also needs good women like you, and that FBI agent."

As Hatch was about to shut the door, Hill caught it with his hand as he rushed up. "I almost forgot to tell you," he said between breaths. "I don't know what she meant by it, but Wendy told me that after-shock was just for you."

Hatch smiled at Hill as she sat in the Rover. She stuck the key in the ignition and took one last look around before she drove away.

Rachel Hatch will returns in Whirlwind. Order your copy of Whirlwind now:
https://www.amazon.com/gp/product/B095PYFF28

Join the LT Ryan reader family & receive a free copy of the Rachel Hatch story, Fractured. Click the link below to get started:
https://ltryan.com/rachel-hatch-newsletter-signup-1

LOVE HATCH? **Noble? Maddie? Cassie?** Get your very own Rachel Hatch merchandise today! Click the link below to find coffee mugs, t-shirts, and even signed copies of your favorite L.T. Ryan thrillers! https://ltryan.ink/EvG_

THE RACHEL HATCH SERIES

Join the LT Ryan reader family & receive a free copy of the Rachel Hatch story, Fractured. Click the link below to get started:

https://ltryan.com/rachel-hatch-newsletter-signup-1

Love Hatch? Noble? Maddie? Cassie? Get your very own Rachel Hatch merchandise today! Click the link below to find coffee mugs, t-shirts, and even signed copies of your favorite L.T. Ryan thrillers! https://ltryan.ink/EvG_

WHIRLWIND CHAPTER 1

Evelyn Mann took two steps inside the general store and stopped, allowing herself a moment to shake off the chill of the late spring morning. The phone had rung three times in less than ten minutes. The first call had been from the school principal informing her that her fifteen-year-old son, Trevor—a sophomore at Hawk's Landing High, and a permanent member of the principal's detention club—had had a behavioral outburst.

The principal hemmed and hawed his way through retelling what had happened. Trevor had flipped his desk when they confiscated his cell phone. His behavior during English class earned him a two-day suspension. Mann pleaded for leniency, but the principal held his ground, further explaining her son's Individualized Education Plan, his IEP. Her son had anger mitigation strategies to avoid outbursts, but when disruption was deemed "beyond mitigation," or, as Mann interpreted it, "beyond wanting to help at the moment," the plan of action was to send him home.

This would be the third time this year her son had been sent home. Mann had to be prepared for any disruptions in his schedule or other-wise. For the next two days, until the weekend hit, she would be on high alert to make sure that none of the inconsistencies of his daily routine would trigger another emotional breakdown. Great! She'd wanted to scream but opted for a frustrated sigh and a promise to pick him up within the next half hour.

Before she had stuffed her phone back into her purse, it rang again. The next incoming call was her ex-husband, a man who always seemed to time when Mann felt her lowest and find a way to make it worse.

Her high-school-sweetheart-turned-cheating-bastard left town over three years ago and in that time had barely made contact with his son, aside from a random phone call. Out of sight for over three years, only stopping by two Christmases ago and even then, he neglected to bring a gift.

Mann wasn't about taking handouts, but she'd reasoned guys like Chad were why deadbeat laws were established in the first place. She'd stayed home to raise their son with Asperger's. Before the diagnosis was made, he was a challenging baby and toddler, to say the least. Not that she had much of a career, but she was working her way to manager at the diner.

When they'd married, Chad had a decent job at the engineering company until they parted ways when he found a younger model with less baggage. He called at various times from different numbers, often switching carriers and numbers without telling her for several months' This, of course, made it impossible for Trevor to speak with his father even if he wanted to. Most of the time, he did not.

But here he was, calling as he always would after any type of issue with Trevor, as if her parenting wasn't enough. Maybe it wasn't, but damn it! He had left her high and dry and now he was two months late on child support.

Although she never used the money as a source of punishment, she wanted to. Hoping to sever any financial strings attached to the divorce, she'd applied for an assistant baker position. As of right now, she was late for the interview. She'd tried to call her potential employer, but the school interrupted, so here she was. Taking a moment to compose herself and shake off the cold, she now had to stare at the ringing phone from her ex-husband. He would call her again and again until she answered. He always did.

She entered the grocery store and noticed the bakery section was on the far right. Mann saw the head baker was busy with an older gentleman at the counter. While Mann made her way over, she decided to answer the call and put a quick end to whatever he was calling for.

"Chad," she said, her tone quiet but harsh. "I don't want to hear it. I'm not in the mood and I'm late for a job interview."

"Whoa, babe. Why do you always gotta give me such a hard time? How come I can't just call and check in?"

"Because you never call and check in. We have to track you down. I'm just shocked that this is the same number you called me from last time."

"Listen, I know I've been spotty with the paychecks, but I was just calling to tell you I'm getting it to you soon."

"Do you know how many times I've heard that? 'Don't worry about it. It's just around the corner,' you'll take care of everything, you'll make things right? Blah, blah, blah. I'm done with it, Chad. I don't need you or your money anymore. I don't need you to remember Trevor's birthday, which you've forgotten the last two years. We don't need you. There was a time when we did. There was a time when you were my world, and I thought everything was right, and now that I see you for who you are, I couldn't be happier that you're gone.

"And trust me, Trevor's going through a tough time. I know you called to rub it in and you're twisting it now like you always do. But let me tell you this, Trevor's going to be fine, too. We need to rid ourselves of the baggage holding us back, and that's you. After this call, the next thing you'll hear is from my attorney and I will get full custody of our son until he turns eighteen. But you will no longer be a part of our lives. Do you understand me?"

"Sure, but you talk like this a lot, too. Always threatening me. Why do you think I have to switch phones so much? Why do I have to change addresses?"

"Because you can't hold a job, Chad. Not since you left." Silence for a moment.

Mann could tell her words hit the mark. He was probably in between jobs now, and he was probably calling just before this cell carrier dropped him, just like a few months back. It was always the same story, shrouded in the same lie. The difference in the man she'd fallen for at sixteen, now thirty-nine, was day and night.

"Goodbye Chad. You're free of us now." Mann clicked "end" on the phone and slid it back into her purse as she moved towards the bakery. She recognized the old man at the counter chatting the baker's ear off. It was her son's psychologist, Glenn Miller. He'd been a godsend for Trevor. They'd only started a few months back, but she'd seen a dramatic improvement in her son's ability to control his outbursts. Miller recently offered to try Trevor on hypnotherapy, something the psychologist claimed to have worked in the past with tremendous results. The irony was not lost on Mann that she was now standing behind him after receiving the call from the school. Something that would no doubt be addressed in Trevor's next session.

Mann checked her watch. It was just a few minutes past nine. She hoped her interview with the baker moved along quicker than the conversation he was having with Miller. Making eye contact with the baker, she smiled. He gave a subtle nod toward Miller, which Mann took to mean: "Whenever Mr. Miller is done, we'll proceed with the interview."

Mann felt her phone vibrating once again. Unzipping her purse, she looked down. It was Chad again. Since hanging up on him she had missed three calls. Now she ignored it once more and zipped her purse back up.

She wasn't kidding this time. She was done with him, done with the games. She wouldn't call him back again and she'd honor her word as she'd meant to time and time again. Mann was deep in thought when someone bumped her from behind, almost knocking her purse off her shoulder.

Mann turned to see the vacant stare of a messy haired kid only a few years older than her son. Rail thin, he wore a short-sleeved white button-up and matching colored pants. Even his lace-less sneakers were white. The boy's attire reminded Mann of the milkmen of old.

The boy in white stopped a foot behind Miller. She listened close and could hear him speaking, but Mann couldn't make it out over the sound of Miller's voice. He mumbled the same word over and over.

Staring at the odd young man, she noticed his right hand. At first, she thought it was an oversized cell phone like the ones you'd see in the 80s, and then she realized the large black item in his hand was a pistol.

The boy continued muttering as he raised the weapon and pointed it at the center of Miller's back.

Mann watched in horror as the first shot rang out. She stood frozen as Miller fell face first onto the floor. The boy fired the gun five more times. He stood rigid, the gun still pointing at the lifeless body of her son's psychologist. His finger continued to pull the trigger of the empty revolver.

Click...click...click.

Mann fled out of the store, into the parking lot where the other employees and patrons had gathered. Sirens could be heard in the distance.

She could see through the front window that the boy in white had not moved. In her head she could still hear the rhythmic strike of the revolver's hammer into the empty cylinder.

Click...click...click.

WHIRLWIND CHAPTER 2

Hatch stood a few feet from the long, parallel steel bars set at chest height. The bars extended for about fifteen feet and marked the start point to the Basic Underwater Demolition SEAL training obstacle course.

Working her arms in small circles to warm up her shoulders, she bent and flexed her knees as Banyan set out the rules for the course.

"Timer starts as soon as you touch the bars. You get two tries on every obstacle. Fail the second time and it's a no-go. Every time you go over the Hooyah logs, you need to interlace your fingers behind your head. When you get to the forty-foot tower, it's your choice how to descend. First phase you have to go feet first, but after that, you can ranger crawl it."

Hatch scanned the expanse of the sandy beach. Unlike Nasty Nick, tucked deep into the North Carolina woods, its obstacles obscured by high trees, she could see all the obstacles before her. It was intimidating when trying to look at everything, so Hatch focused on the first task.

"Once the timer starts, you have twelve minutes to complete all eleven obstacles and get back here."

Hatch nodded. What started over beers would end here on the

sand. She checked the laces on her boots and tucked her BDU pants inside. She wore a long-sleeved shirt and they gave her the option of wearing a shock resistant helmet, but she opted not to.

Hatch stood ready, tuning out the back-and-forth trash talking between Banyan and Cruise. A light mist descended as Hatch gripped the parallel bars. She knew the timer on Banyan's watch had started, and so had the one running in her own head.

She hoisted herself onto the bars. Bicycling her legs, she shimmied across the fifteen feet to the other side quickly. Approaching the low wall, she used the stump in front of it to vault over to the high wall. The high wall's wood surface was already coated in the mist and the wood was now slick to the touch, too high for Hatch to jump over the seven-foot-two wall, but it had a thick rope hanging at its center.

Hatch gave a two-step lunge, grabbing the rope midway and pulling herself up and over the wall. The light rain dampened the sand and kept it from getting in her face and eyes as she dropped to her belly and began low crawling under the barbed wire. Pulling herself through the sandy pit, she faced off with a fifty-foot cargo net.

Though she had faced her fear of heights at her father's hand, time and time again during her service in the military, and most recently on an Alaskan mountaintop, Hatch still had to face the same fear every time. Each time, she had to find her workaround for coping.

She'd had plenty of experience with the cargo net. Eyes straight ahead, look at the rope right in front of you. And she did, ascending one of the cargo lines, using the vertical knots in front of her as her handholds, taking two or three rungs at a time with her feet. She ascended the fifty feet and then hoisted herself over the other side, trying to keep her head upright, looking at the horizon. She made quick work to the bottom.

A zigzag of uneven bars rolled, but Hatch moved fast and maintained her balance. She felt she was making good time as she did a rope exchange, climbing one twelve-foot rope and then reaching across to descend on another. Her gut was tested on an obstacle known as the Ugly Name.

She had to jump from one horizontal timber to another. The second timber was a few feet higher and several feet further. She saw the only way to effectively go over the higher log was to jump hard and take the impact at the waist, which Hatch did. The thick log's curved side slammed hard into her stomach, causing her to curse as she rolled her body forward and over the painful obstacle.

She navigated the Weaver with relative ease, the staple obstacle of many courses she'd run before. She then encountered another set of the Hooyah logs. The stack of logs rising five timbers high were staggered throughout. She used it to catch her breath before encountering the next obstacle.

The Burma Bridge had a twenty-foot rope hanging down on one end. Hatch ascended it and came to a three-rope bridge where the knots between the connections widened as the bridge extended across the sand. Hatch used her long legs to her advantage as she crossed the bridge.

On the other side, she looked at the obstacle awaiting her, the Forty-Foot Tower, a four-story wooden structure open on all sides. At the very top, a long thick rope extended down to the sand at a forty-five-degree angle. Hatch jogged up on the obstacle and took a moment to catch her breath. Her arms and legs burned. A metallic taste filled her mouth and she spit it into the wet sand.

Hatch reached up. The lip of the first tier was just out of reach. Hatch would have to jump and then swing her leg on the outside. With the soft sand slightly packed from the rain, she bent her legs and sprung up. Gripping hard with her left hand and digging her fingernails into the wood, she kicked her left leg up hard and over, using the momentum of her jump. She clawed her way onto the first level of the tower.

Now, inside the tower structure, she had to reach out. Again, she could only touch the bottom, not the top lip. She positioned herself at the edge, keeping her left hand ready. And just like on the ground, she bent her knees and shot up, grabbing at the rung.

She kicked her leg hard. The side of her boot hit the outside wood, knocking her off balance. Her fingers slipped. She let go and tried to catch herself on the first level, but fell back-flat onto the packed sand below. The impact knocked the wind out of Hatch.

She exhaled. Rolling to her side, she punched the sand, angry at herself. She took two short breaths in, clearing her mind, and reset at the base of the tower. Just like she had done before, she navigated to the first level. This time, Hatch made sure not to underestimate the effort needed to get beyond.

Everything grew quiet. Her only focus was on the floor just above her. Hatch bent deep and then shot her arm upwards, kicking hard and wide. The momentum carried her up and over. Her left arm fatigued from the effort. She switched to her right side. Hatch repeated the process, lunging to the third floor. She felt the tingle in her scarred right arm as she worked her way to her knees.

The fourth and final tier that would take her to the top of the tower required her to go through an open shoot door at the top. To do so, Hatch had to jump and catch the upper lip of the top tier with both elbows, then swing her bent knee through. Catching herself with her heels, she rolled to the right.

On her knees, at the top of the forty-foot tower, the wind from the Pacific Ocean just beyond the high sand berms pushed a breeze across. Hatch worked herself over on her hands and knees to the rope extending down. She lay belly flat on the wet wood surface and pulled herself out.

As her right knee came off the top landing of the tower, she draped her ankle across the wire rope, stabilizing herself as she descended. Her left leg hung loose and acted as a counterbalance to the shifts of her body weight. Hatch made quick work getting to the bottom. The remaining obstacles posed little challenge in the way of difficulty.

Her biggest hurdle behind her, Hatch now focused on time as she crossed a rope swing, moved across a set of monkey bars, navigated a short obstacle hurdle, and then used her fingertips and the edges of her boot to scale a spider wall before dropping into a dead sprint across the sand to the finish line where Banyan and Cruise waited.

As Hatch ran to the two, Banyan called time. Hatch dropped her hands to her knees and took two big inhales. "How'd I do?" Hatch gasped between ragged breaths.

"8:34," Banyan said, looking at his watch.

Cruise held out his hand. "Pay up. A bet's a bet."

Words had obviously been exchanged during Hatch's navigation of the obstacle course. This was evident by the roll of Banyan's eyes as he fished out his wallet.

"Banyan's just mad because you almost beat his best time."

Banyan's face reddened.

"Not everyone runs it in six minutes." Cruise tapped the cane against his braced right leg, the damage done during their last op in Alaska. "I think those days are long gone. I'm not an Honor Man like you."

"Those days are never gone."

"But come to think of it, I'll take you on a double or nothing."

Banyan ran his thumb across the money in his billfold and cocked a curious eye at Cruise.

"I bet Hatch here can best your time. Shoot, all she has to do is drop two seconds. If she hadn't fallen off that second tier of the tower, she would've had you."

"Whoa!" Hatch threw up her hands, taking a big inhale of the cool morning air. "Who said I'd ever run that thing again? Remember, this all started because you guys wanted to know which obstacle course was tougher."

"And the verdict?" Banyan asked.

"Nasty Nick is everything as nasty as they say. But if I'm being honest, this course provides some X factors I've never seen anywhere else. The sand makes it a totally different challenge. And that tower almost got me."

"About that," Banyan said. "You tried to go up by swinging your leg to the side. A lot of guys do it, but there's an easier way. Not all of us are tall drinks of water like your friend Cruise here. Guys like me, in the Smurf crew, we had to adapt and overcome."

Banyan was four inches shorter than Hatch, so about five-foot-six. "The way to do it with minimal effort and best success is to start deeper, underneath each tier, and jump and grab with both hands on the lip, swinging your legs underneath you, using the momentum of both legs to pull you up and over, like an intense kip-up."

"I'll keep it in mind. But as of right now, don't bet on me running this again."

Cruise opened his mouth to speak when the cell phone in his hand vibrated. He'd been holding it for Hatch and handed it to her. She flicked it open.

"It's Tracy."

The message from Jordan Tracy, Talon Executive Services Commander, read, "Brief at ten?"

Hatch messaged back, "RGR."

She looked up at Cruise. "Briefing at ten."

"Oh, the Bat signal has sounded. Don't want to keep you from your secret lair," Banyan cut in.

"Banyan's not a big fan of private contract work. He'd rather help midlife crisis males and overweight homebodies try to get their SEAL shape on." Cruise teased.

"Hey." Banyan raised his hand in defense. "I'm doing my part to make people at the beaches look better. It's a public service, really. The world can thank me later."

Cruise looked at his watch and then checked his phone.

"No message?" Hatch asked.

He shook his head no. "Strange."

Hatch got another message. It was the name of a café. "Stranger, the briefing is not at the office."

Banyan pulled out his money to pay his bet. Cruise put his hand out, refusing it. "I'd still like to keep the double or nothing on the table."

"Keep it on the table all you want," Hatch said. "You're not getting me back on that tower."

WHIRLWIND CHAPTER 3

The pen stopped where it always did. The part where he started to write the three words he'd never had the heart to say but always wished he had. For spending such little time with someone, he had never thought about anyone more in his life. As he set the pen down, this would be another letter to Rachel Hatch that he never finished.

He sipped his coffee. Hatch's mother, Jasmine, had made him a thermos-full when he had stopped by earlier that morning to check on the kids and say, "Hi." Something he did whenever he was close, and sometimes when he wasn't. In the absences between Hatch's comings and goings, he had taken on the role of surrogate father or uncle for the kids, and Jasmine Hatch doted on him like a son.

Savage set the letter aside on his desk. He traded his pen for the thermos and took a long pull of Jasmine's brew.

His cell phone rang as his radio came to life. The radio always took priority. When he had taken over as Sheriff of Hawk's Landing, he said that both his cell and radio would be accessible twenty-four hours a day.

"Sheriff Savage? Sheriff Savage, are you there?" He had tried to get everybody in his small department onto a code system similar to the one Denver PD used, but it hadn't taken.

"Go ahead Barbara. What do you got?" Savage said, draining the last of his coffee, figuring this call would take him late into the night.

"It's at Westin's Grocery. Some crazy with a gun went in and shot Glenn Miller. I mean, somebody shot to death a 72-year-old man standing in a grocery store! This is Hawk's Landing, not Los Angeles!" Her voice was on edge.

"Barbara, I need you to tell me, where is the shooter now? What's the situation on scene at this moment?"

"Chaos. But the caller I spoke with said he fired the gun until empty, but he didn't take aim at anyone else. And he didn't run."

"He's still on scene?"

"Caller said he's standing there with the gun in his hand. He hasn't moved."

"Is anybody else hurt or wounded?"

"No. An older woman was knocked down as shoppers fled."

Savage was already in his SUV and speeding toward town center where the Westin's was located. "Besides Miller and the shooter, is there anybody else still inside?"

"No. I've got the caller on the line and will keep you posted."

Savage keyed the mic. "Sinclair, did you copy?"

"Already on my way." Sirens blared in the background.

"As long as the shooter remains inside and there are no other reports of gunfire, you hold on the outside and wait for me before entering."

"Yessir."

"The second that changes and the shooting becomes active again, you're going in. With or without me. Understood?"

"Yessir." This time, her voice was less resolute.

"Hold the perimeter. And whatever you do, do not let him leave." Tires squealed as he took a hard right. "I'm on my way."

Savage tore down the winding mountain roads and headed into the downtown area of Hawk's Landing. As he turned onto Main Street, he could see the siren lights flickering. He navigated his way around some pedestrian bystanders looking on from a distance and found a spot next to Sinclair's squad car. She was standing outside with her gun in front of her, pointing to the storefront.

There was no sign of the man with the gun, but they maintained a loosely held perimeter out of the sheer fear and panic of the moment. Savage walked toward it all. He never ran, always taking his steps carefully to process the scene, making sure the shooter hadn't slipped out and pretended to be a bystander. He made sure there was no odd man out. Seeing none, he proceeded to Sinclair's position.

"Nothing?"

"Nothing since the call came in."

"We need to move in now. We have to open the line of communication and render lifesaving aid to the downed man."

"But the shooter killed him. "

"I don't care if they shot him with a bazooka. Until I confirm life or death, I'm assuming he's alive, and we're going to try to bring him out as such."

"Understood, sir."

"Stack up. We're moving."

Savage and Sinclair pressed forward, moving with their weapons tight against their chests, sighted in the direction of the known threat. Sirens bounced off the neighboring buildings as Littleton's squad car screeched to a halt on the other side of the road. The lanky deputy sprinted awkwardly toward them and joined their gaggle just as they entered the store.

An eerie silence cast out the chaos of the terrified citizenry on the outside of the doors. Soft elevator music played over a PA system. They moved slowly, using the aisles for cover. Savage at the lead, he cleared each one before stepping to the next, moving ever closer to the bakery area.

He moved soft shoe, rolling his heel along the outside to his toes, a trick he'd learned from one of his partners who'd done a stint in the military He could hear Littleton and Sinclair trying, but failing, to move noiselessly behind him, into the last barrier where aisle one and two divided.

He leaned against the fresh garden veggies open refrigeration unit and could feel the cool blast of mist showering the produce. Through the baker's door across the way, Savage glimpsed the shooter in the reflection of the glass. He stood still in a white short-sleeve button-up and white denim pants. He was looking forward and down, the opposite direction from Savage and his team.

Savage held his non-gun hand behind his head and began a countdown with his fingers: *three, two, one.*

He stepped wide, bringing the weapon up to target and began barking orders in a loud, controlled tone.

"You in the white shirt, drop the weapon. This is Dalton Savage, Hawk's Landing Sheriff. I have three guns trained on you. We do not want to hurt you!"

Nothing. Silence. Except for the repetitive click of the trigger.

The shooter continued looking down at the floor, soaked slick with Glenn Miller's blood. There was no doubt Miller was dead from the amount of blood spreading out. Rendering aid was a moot point. Surviving the deadly encounter now took precedent.

"Drop the gun. Now!" Simple commands, simple words.

Sinclair shifted her position and stumbled. She knocked into a rack of potato chips, sending the rack and its contents to the floor. The loud bang of the metal hitting against the hard floor, startled the shooter. Like a starter pistol, the boy in white seemed to come out of a trance, looking around as if he'd just woken from a nightmare.

His stunned gaze shifted from Sinclair as she recovered to lock eyes with Savage.

Savage saw a fleeting look of horror on the young face. The weapon fell from his hand and clattered loudly to the floor beside him.

In the minutes that followed, while Savage's team took the shooter into custody, the boy didn't utter a single word. Savage looked through the rear window of Sinclair's cruiser, noticing the white clothing dotted with the spatter of Miller's blood.

The young shooter sat with his back rigid and stared ahead at the wired cage separating him from the vehicle's front compartment. Only his trigger finger moved, rhythmically tapping his knee.

Tap...tap...tap.

Rachel Hatch will returns in Whirlwind. Order your copy of Whirlwind now:

https://www.amazon.com/gp/product/B095PYFF28

Join the LT Ryan reader family & receive a free copy of the Rachel Hatch story, Fractured. Click the link below to get started: https://ltryan.com/rachel-hatch-newsletter-signup-1

ALSO BY L.T. RYAN

Find All of L.T. Ryan's Books on Amazon Today!

The Jack Noble Series

The Recruit (free)

The First Deception (Prequel 1)

Noble Beginnings

A Deadly Distance

Ripple Effect (Bear Logan)

Thin Line

Noble Intentions

When Dead in Greece

Noble Retribution

Noble Betrayal

Never Go Home

Beyond Betrayal (Clarissa Abbot)

Noble Judgment

Never Cry Mercy

Deadline

End Game

Noble Ultimatum

Noble Legend

Noble Revenge

Never Look Back (Coming Soon)

Bear Logan Series

Ripple Effect

Blowback

Take Down

Deep State

Bear & Mandy Logan Series

Close to Home

Under the Surface

The Last Stop

Over the Edge

Between the Lies (Coming Soon)

Rachel Hatch Series

Drift

Downburst

Fever Burn

Smoke Signal

Firewalk

Whitewater

Aftershock

Whirlwind

Tsunami

Fastrope

Sidewinder (Coming Soon)

Mitch Tanner Series

The Depth of Darkness

Into The Darkness

Deliver Us From Darkness

Cassie Quinn Series

Path of Bones

Whisper of Bones

Symphony of Bones

Etched in Shadow

Concealed in Shadow

Betrayed in Shadow

Born from Ashes

Blake Brier Series

Unmasked

Unleashed

Uncharted

Drawpoint

Contrail

Detachment

Clear

Quarry (Coming Soon)

Dalton Savage Series

Savage Grounds

Scorched Earth

Cold Sky

The Frost Killer (Coming Soon)

Maddie Castle Series

The Handler

Tracking Justice

Hunting Grounds (Coming Soon)

Affliction Z Series

Affliction Z: Patient Zero

Affliction Z: Abandoned Hope

Affliction Z: Descended in Blood

Affliction Z : Fractured Part 1

Affliction Z: Fractured Part 2 (Fall 2021)

Love Hatch? Noble? Maddie? Cassie? Get your very own L.T. Ryan merchandise today! Click the link below to find coffee mugs, t-shirts, and even signed copies of your favorite thrillers! https://ltryan.ink/EvG_

Receive a free copy of The Recruit. Visit:

https://ltryan.com/jack-noble-newsletter-signup-1

ABOUT THE AUTHOR

L.T. Ryan is a *USA Today* and international bestselling author. The new age of publishing offered L.T. the opportunity to blend his passions for creating, marketing, and technology to reach audiences with his popular Jack Noble series.

Living in central Virginia with his wife, the youngest of his three daughters, and their three dogs, L.T. enjoys staring out his window at the trees and mountains while he should be writing, as well as reading, hiking, running, and playing with gadgets. See what he's up to at http://ltryan.com.

Social Medial Links:

- Facebook (L.T. Ryan): https://www.facebook.com/LTRyanAuthor

- Facebook (Jack Noble Page): https://www.facebook.com/JackNobleBooks/

- Twitter: https://twitter.com/LTRyanWrites

- Goodreads: http://www.goodreads.com/author/show/6151659.L_T_Ryan

Made in the USA
Monee, IL
09 November 2023

46142727R00132